FIELDS OF MADNESS

John Cooper

Published by New Generation Publishing in 2022

First Edition

ISBN: 978-1-80369-244-9

www.newgeneration-publishing.com

New Generation Publishing

CHAPTER 1

Had he not taken up shooting, Nathan Chalmers would never have discovered his talents as a peacemaker. Nor would he have volunteered as a guinea pig for experimental brain surgery. It was his search for something to temper the stress of solving problems no one else could handle that got him to join a shoot. That was the burden of becoming one of the industry's acknowledged geniuses where complex software was concerned. Nathan just didn't understand the meaning of "insoluble".

This morning, he boiled a free-range egg for roughly five minutes and followed it with a bowl of muesli while scanning yesterday's mail. He didn't open any envelopes that looked as though they might carry advertisements. He chucked them onto the window sill where they remained for a week or so. Then he would bin them. Today, having eaten, he dressed for a day on the moor in the outfit inherited from his father. Tweed jacket and breaches, Tattersal check shirt and a tie with the silhouette of two retrievers. He enjoyed the rituals of shooting, even though he was no marksman. He loved to see the party ranged over the moor, the beaters in the distance advancing towards the butts with their dogs bursting for a chance to show their skills. He jumped into his top-of-the-range Volvo and after a leisurely hour's drive, he met up with other guns. He declined a glass of port, made sure his name was in the draw for butts, then clambered into the club's van for the rough ride over the moorland to the site of the first drive. It was a great day for shooting. Bright sky, a steady breeze and air that made his lungs sing with joy.

Later, he tried to condense all he had learned about shooting game birds, in preparation for the next drive. After three years as a member of the shoot, he was still trying to fit together what was most important. Left foot forward, shotgun loaded and ready to swing onto the line of flight of the quarry, and then waiting to pull the trigger until he had the correct lead distance on the fast moving bird. Today, as the beaters flushed the grouse from the heather, the birds came on fast and low, missiles in loose formation, splitting their lines for Russian roulette over the butts. Shots and the sniff of cordite soured the moorland air. Ten birds dropped. The rest vanished over the heather to live another week.

It was over in seconds. Demoralised, Nathan broke open the double barrelled Springfield. Spent cartridges added to the pile at his feet. A Smart Alec in the next butt, whose single shot had downed one of the birds, threw him a condescending smirk.

"I think you scared one of the buggers then," he called in a throaty and clearly audible voice.

Yet to hit anything in the first three drives of the day, with Nathan once again in the same embarrassing position, he began to seriously consider resigning from the shoot to find a pastime which didn't make him feel inadequate. Then, in the relative calm following the drive, as pickers-up worked with the dogs to retrieve the kills, an argument erupted between two of the guns further down the line. A loud mouthed occupant of the butts was taking exception to one of his neighbours, clad in mustard coloured tweeds of distinct flamboyance.

"You total cretin...you complete arsehole... you'll bloody well kill somebody before the day's out..."

"Shut your dirty mouth you son-of-a-bitch or I'll stuff that gun up your ass..."

The first voice was North Country, the second unmistakably transatlantic. Dennis Drewery, the shoot manager, arrived before the quarrel escalated. He saw the two men, in adjacent butts, were angry enough to brawl.

"Gentlemen! Please! Now what's happened here? Calm down and let's sort this out. I don't want to have to send you off the moor."

Dennis, with thirty years experience of managing shooting parties, was firm. He had dealt with these situations occasionally when rigid protocol had been breached. Disputes were common now the Estate was obliged to rely upon nouveau riche Brits or wealthy visitors from overseas, whose shooting skills and etiquette were sometimes incompatible. The culture of British game shooting was alien to them. Dennis's job was to ensure all members of each party enjoyed a safe day's sport, were impressed with the numbers of birds presented, and rewarded with a satisfactory "bag".

The man who had complained was still bristling: "It's Davy Crockett here. He swung straight through the line. I didn't get off a shot. I was frightened of getting my bleedin' head blown off. He's an absolute menace. It's not the first time he's done it. I'm not entering another butt anywhere near this pillock."

The American, livid at the Davy Crockett slur, waved a fist and faced the manager: "Is this how you treat guests? Standing them in line with idiots? I did take a high bird behind the butts but it was a safe shot. The barrels were vertical when I turned through the line."

Nathan, diffident by nature, decided that some intervention was needed. Scratching his fingers through his hair, he slowly walked over and spoke to the American in quiet, mediatory tones: "If Mr. Drewery doesn't object, I'll take the butt adjoining yours on the next drive." Then, ignoring the irate loudmouth and turning to the shoot manager, "Will that be OK with you, Dennis?"

Unflappable and in no rush to continue until he was sure there would be no further trouble, the shoot manager looked long into the face of each man. When he judged that they had both cooled down, he said firmly, "If there should be any further arguments, I am afraid that means I will have to ask you both to leave the moor. You must remain calm with safety uppermost in your mind. Accidents in field sports are caused by those who forget that."

The arrangement was accepted and the rest of the day passed with everyone being extravagantly careful. Nathan even managed a few half decent shots, to the approval of the American. Eventually it came time for the party to check their guns were empty before they boarded the transport for the journey down from the moor. Nathan sat with the American in the van as it made a bouncy return to the main road and back to the Estate dining room for supper. Although the loud mouth had said nothing further to the American, he was taken to one side, given a brace of grouse and invited to leave before supper. Here again, it was Nathan's discreet suggestion that had been acted upon. Better, he thought, to get the aggrieved "gun" out of the way before alcohol could fuel further abuse.

At supper, the American was charming in his praise of Nathan's behaviour. "I like the way you sorted that thing out young man. You might even have the credentials for a place in our diplomatic service if you ever want to change career," he said light-heartedly. And then, "What do you do? For a profession I mean. Are you on the staff of the Estate?"

Nathan received the praise with a shrug. He put down the glass of red and pushed himself back in his chair. He fleetingly reviewed why he had taken to game shooting and why, today, he had practically made up his mind to pack it in.

"I've had a gun in this shoot for a few years but I've nothing to do with the Estate. I can easily afford it and I did see it as the ideal counter balance to debugging computer software, which is the day job. I am a partner in what we claim is the UK's top IT consultancy. I work with all the biggest names in commerce. Quite stressful, but it's what I'm good at. It's great up there on the moors, out in the wild, when you've been cooped in an office sorting out software malfunctions. I'm a useless shot. I don't mind missing birds but I loathe wounding them."

"You don't say," said the American, "I know what you're talking about. I'm in computers myself."

The pair jawed amicably throughout supper much of the time about the latest developments in software for IT. Afterwards, the American, who had not given away a great deal about his business, offered Nathan his card. "Sal Goering, President, Bagnold Medical Sciences Inc, N.J." Then he made the offer.

"I got a massive problem right now on a major new product launch. We've millions of bucks tied up in the project but my trouble shooters have hit bedrock. They seem to think the problem's insoluble. What say I fly you over to the States next week and you sit in on one of our development meetings?" As Nathan didn't respond immediately, the American gave him a piercing stare then he added, "Money no object!"

The young computer ace wasn't a gambler and he was a meticulous guardian of his privacy and working hours. Though as a consultant, he had to grab opportunities for fee earning when they came along.

"Can I give it some serious thought this weekend and get back to you Monday?" he asked.

"Do that," Sal replied, his face forming into a rigid smile, "take all the time you need. Then phone me tomorrow - or not at all..."

CHAPTER 2

Bagnold Medical Science
Confidential memorandum from the desk of the President
To Cyrus Blatt, Vice President, Global marketing.
Status: most urgent

I have just returned from the UK, where I met someone who could be useful in finding a solution to the glitch on Neuro-Praxis. Trouble-shooting is his speciality and my pals over there have him down as the top gun. I want you to let him look at the programme to see if he has an answer to the hold up. As Mogdanowicz and Seimens seem incapable of sorting things out, maybe the Brit can do something with it. I have not settled a fee but you can pay him whatever he wants. His name is Nathan Chalmers. My secretary has his full contact details. Fly him in first class – immediately. I will talk to him after you and your team have seen him.

Bagnold Medical Sciences
Confidential Memorandum from Vice President, Global Marketing
F.A.O. the President
Status: strictly confidential

Your request actioned today. Chalmers arrives tomorrow. I am paying him top dollar; your judgement is always good. I just have to sell it to Mogdanowicz and Seimens.

***

Nathan chucked his grip on the king size bed and surveyed the room. Bagnold did not scrimp on cost. As well as the en-suite bathroom and generous lounge area, there were mirror faced sliding doors which glided back to reveal a few metres of hanging space and umpteen shelves in solid beech - far too grand for the clean underwear, three shirts and spare slacks which made up the contents of his bag.

He poured himself a juice from the mini-bar and, selecting a comfortable armchair, picked up the remote and surfed the giant TV for something to relax him after the flight. As he sipped the ice cold mango drink, he began thinking about Koley, the Product manager sent to greet him at the airport. He had never experienced such an emotional and physical shock since he was selected to open the batting for his college at university, and was out first ball for a duck. Koley made a stunning entrance to his life. A tall redhead, black suit sculpted to her body, stiletto heels that accentuated long shapely legs, and movement like a super model on the catwalk. In his jet lagged state, he was quite incapable of absorbing anything other than her physical presence.

'They don't lose any time, these Yanks', he mused. Though as he found Koley rated highest ever on his personal sex appeal thermometer, he didn't mind jumping fast out of the blocks. He had never really developed any sort of technique with women. Having not the slightest clue on how to attempt a conquest, he normally waited to see what happened. Usually, nothing. Charles Colquhoun, the closest person he had to a genuine friend in the consultancy, had put into words. He made up a vulgar rhyme and stuck it on the staff notice board – so much more effective than burying it on a chat line.

Nathan knew that he was not greatly attractive to women. One of the reasons was probably his lack of fashion sense. When he bought clothes, he was more concerned with getting the correct size, irrespective of such considerations as suitability for his build, design and colour. As a result, he never appeared to be either badly dressed or well dressed. He was just "clothed", usually according to the season. He did have dates, women choosing him by that intuitive process which can identify someone who won't give them any trouble. However, because they chose him and not vice versa, they were never really suitable partners. What he craved was a woman whose intelligence he respected, one who could hold her own in the male dominated world of I.T. In short, he fancied someone like Koley, the redhead with the Harvard degree who made his temperature rise when she sat with him in the back of the limousine on the way from the airport. Without much prompting, she had told him about herself. It was in response to his raised eyebrows at the declaration of her unusual name.

“I was Christened Columbine because my mum was a thespian obsessed with the Commedia dell’arte. When I got to High School, it was shortened to Collie by the other girls. It sounded too much like a dog or a vegetable so my friends and I compromised on ‘Koley’ and it’s been that ever since.”

“I suppose if you had a brother, he would have been called Harlequin,” said Nathan, attempting to show his awareness of the Commedia dell’arte reference with light humour.

“I do have a younger brother, Peregrine, but everyone calls him Perry,” she replied airily.

Koley was quite happy to talk about herself on the journey. Nathan realised that she had reached the stage of her career where the ‘must have’ material possessions were already hers, including the apartment in the city. It was completely over his head that her clothes showed an understanding of what female middle management should wear in New York to tread the fine line between status statement and provocation. Nathan thought her masculine hair style exaggerated rather than reduced her femininity. She was a beautifully presented woman with high cheek bones, full lips and faultless poise. Although everyone she met always remembered the assets of her soft caramel voice and her dramatic bright green eyes.

Side by side in the car, he had been immediately drawn to her but without any idea how to make an advance. He did not have the confidence to suggest a date. As usual, he approached the problem in an obtuse and ineffective way, wondering what she might choose from a menu in an expensive restaurant, instead of simply inviting her for a meal.

He was thinking about his latest encounter as he selected something to view. He didn’t listen to the dialogue, his tired eyes merely watching the screen. He had chosen a favourite American sitcom featuring a divorced psychiatrist. The central character regularly got himself entangled with quite unsuitable women. Nathan smiled as the psychiatrist burst out, “What on earth made you think I would prefer to go to a toga party at your pilates class when we might be dining at Chez Maurice? You must have caught a brain virus from that demented poodle you carry around all day.” The date looked shocked and quickened the stroking of her pet. Nathan closed his eyes.

He awoke an hour later, realising he must take a shower and then read the file Koley had left with him. To his dismay, a working breakfast had been scheduled for 8am next day. He had to get up to speed. It was whilst he luxuriated under the steaming shower that he recalled the dialogue he had heard before he dozed off. A ‘brain virus’? That is what had lodged in his memory and he began to toss the idea around in his mind until he felt he might possibly have a route to a solution to Bagnold’s problem. He was unable to collect his thoughts, being too weary, but his mind still meandered through possibilities. He was amused by the idea that a TV sitcom might have given him a lead. The highly paid trouble shooters at Bagnold had been stuck for weeks and now he began to see a way through the hold up. He came out of the bathroom with his mind refreshed. He picked up the file, placed it on the table and began to read with growing enthusiasm.

CHAPTER 3

The atmosphere was chilly and it was nothing to do with the climate control system. The working breakfast of coffee, juice and pastries was not to Nathan's taste but he bit into a Danish whilst considering his moves. Cyrus Blatt sat at the head of the table. Nathan sensed he had spent time filing his incisors that morning. He did not look at Nathan nor greet him, but glared at Koley. How vulnerable she looked; how she held her cup and sipped the jet black beverage. He had caught a whiff of something expensive as she had passed behind his chair and he liked what it said about her. Unlike Blatt, who wore his masculinity like a badge of office.

The Vice President had spent the first few minutes of the meeting, before Nathan's arrival, outlining the current stage of development on Neuro-Praxis and identifying the effects of the stoppage. He had picked through the status reports of each of the executives. In turn, he had roasted them, offering little encouragement and often straying off business matters onto their personal qualities. Nathan soon formed the opinion that he was the type of bully he had previously encountered in corporate management.

Bagnold, who specialised in software for the neurosurgical market, were at an advanced stage of trialling Neuro-Praxis, their new brain scanning technology. It would be able to read the entire structure of the brain and map it in a neural network using artificially created DNA molecules. Other companies in China and Germany were working on such technology but the unique and sensational aspect of Bagnold's design was that it could "learn" spontaneously and grow without restriction using on-line Internet resources. By mapping the entire structure of the subject's brain, it would have access to all its memories and beliefs. There might well be some high level dispute and differences on what the information sources should be and trawling the Internet through thousands of websites and data warehouses may not be the most efficient route. The core of the neural network was based on a synthesis of quantum computing and bio computing technologies of unimaginable power compared to that available in a digital system.

Bagnold believed they had perfected the software by employing on-line heuristic sources. However, a crisis had arisen when each time an attempt was made to charge it with gamma radiation; the system developed an expanding series of infinite loops, which was the computational equivalent of a neutron bomb!

"Koley sweetheart," Blatt sneered, "is there the slightest goddam chance we can clear this bug – or are those expensive knickers of yours so tightly twisted your vision's impaired? Goddamit! I must have a new strategy before the Board kicks my ass back to a sales rep's job. I have a progress meeting with Goering on Friday and sure as hell, he's not going to like it if we're still stuck at Stage 5 on the launch schedule. All your jobs are at risk."

Koley looked as though she would rather be in Illinois. Her wide mouth attempted a half smile at the wisecrack. It was a failure. She unpursed her lips and prepared to defend her position. Nathan, to his secret embarrassment, had been mentally undressing her for the past ten minutes. Now, he white knighted to the rescue and surprised himself with his authority. Slapping the flat of his hands on the table, hard enough to shock everyone into silence, he looked around the room. With everybody staring at him, he stared back and said nothing. He let them stare, sliding his hands slowly off the table. Six pairs of eyes followed his hands. It was a trick he had borrowed from Charles Colqhoun, an expert showman. Charles had gifted it to Nathan with the rider, "I'll bet you daren't use it." Although Nathan had done so and rather amazed him.

"Cyrus, I am delighted to tell you I have worked out a strategy to get you and your team back on schedule. I just need your backing to proceed."

There was a dumbfounded silence, then, "Don't mess about. What strategy? Have you diagnosed the problem or not...?" A thin veil of aggression cloaked the nervousness in his voice.

Nathan withheld the "yes" or "no" answer he knew they all wanted. Instead, he explained in detail what he intended to attempt. He compared the software to a "primordial soup", containing virus like organisms, some of which were "misbehaving" in transporting DNA molecules. Then, having set the scene and studied the rapt expressions around the table, he lobbed in his bombshell. He intended, he told them, to use his own brain to discover the precise nature of the problem. To achieve this, he would accept a micro-implant, which would enable him to set up a two-way communication with the system.

"Just like Blue Tooth," he said choosing an analogy the suits would understand. From this sensational vantage point, he would penetrate the 'soup' and examine the behaviour of each virus until he could identify the culprit. Once this could be projected to the scanner, it could be zapped using the sanitiser in the software.

The audacity of the proposal stunned the meeting. With a smile, Nathan surveyed the faces, their expressions frozen in disbelief, staring in his direction, waiting for someone to speak. The silence continued until Koley reacted first, bathing him in that caramel voice.

"That's a helluva way to diagnose our problem Nathan. Hands-on is one thing, but brain on..." she hesitated then, "Even if it could work, it's too risky. Couldn't we simulate a brain, a virtual reality product? I'll bet you're brilliant at that."

Nathan glowed, momentarily lost for words. Jumping on the silence and an apparently safe bandwagon, Cyrus threw in,"Why not a troupe of virtuals we could shove in there like a platoon of Navy Seals. Get the job done, maybe without casualties."

Nathan never did do confrontation and wasn't about to start now. He explained the best approach would be "gently-gently" and that he was ninety percent sure he could clear the blockage, but only if the specification of the procedure was observed in fine detail. They would learn nothing by using a simulated brain. He would have to talk to the top neurosurgeon in New York in order to design the sort of implant he had in mind. The surgery would have to be carried out in such a way that, following the attempt at the debugging work, the implant could be plucked out without side effects. The entire plan involved a ground-breaking technique, which would be patented to him, but franchised to Bagnold Medical Science Inc for the purpose of this one exercise. "A detailed plan would take a few weeks", he said.

One of the suits from The Commercial Department made a meal of warning that the lawyers would be generating enormous fees for producing a contract to indemnify the company against any 'unwanted outcome'. However, Cyrus stepped into the challenge immediately and bluntly promised that the lawyers would do as they were told. He glimpsed in the Englishman's radical idea, a solution to the nightmare that had dogged him for months. This was where he excelled, he told himself, taking difficult decisions, steamrollering positive actions through the commercial fairies. He overruled all opposition and even promised to identify the most famous surgeon in New York to meet with Nathan for an early assessment of the surgical challenges.

Within six weeks, precise surgical needs had been defined, indemnities laboriously worded and a state-of-the-art operating theatre in New York selected. When he was satisfied that all eventualities were covered, Nathan underwent the implant. It turned out that Blatt had, indeed, identified the best surgeon for the task. The neurosurgeon had enthusiastically grasped the requirement and had suggested the adaptation of an existing electronic device, normally used to stimulate, with precision, various parts of a defective brain. Almost microscopic in size, the implant was merely the vehicle of communication for transmitting information to Nathan's own brain, which would do the hard work of diagnosing the blockage. The actual surgical procedure was little different to hundreds of cases of neurosurgery taking place every year. Nathan, who had insisted on remaining fully conscious throughout, was able to respond to the surgeon's questions during the operation. The location of the implant was the task which demanded – and attained – total accuracy. After the operation, Nathan felt sublimely supernatural, his mind floating in and out of focus. Though when questions were voiced, he was completely unable to frame a sensible response.

One month after the surgery, comforted and almost hero-worshipped by Koley, having given time for the implant to settle down and undergo working trials, he again engaged with the network. It was an unworldly experience with Nathan, horizontal on a surgical bed, surrounded by IT technical personnel hanging on to his every word. Initially, what he said was gobbledegook and the faint hearts were quick with their knowing looks. Hadn't they always thought it was a crazy idea?

Koley, worried that Nathan would suffer permanent harm, managed to hold her silence. It was decided that he would rest for a week and then try again. Yet within 48 hours, he suddenly seemed back to normal. He was keen to make another attempt but a few hours each day doing crossword puzzles with Koley convinced him his best course was to take a full week. The surgeon now took some convincing to subject the patient to the ordeal of neurosurgery yet again. However, he eventually agreed to go ahead under a stipulation that it would be his final attempt. Once into the procedure, Nathan's language gradually lost its rambling confusion and began to make sense. A noise emerged from him which could not be confused with any other sound. It was a loud chuckle. Six pairs of eyes widened as they stared at a smiling Englishman. Then Nathan revealed the reason for his amusement. He explained what he had found. It was a rogue gene, which Nathan likened to a teenage girl, who was perfectly sweet most of the time until, without warning, she gave out unpredictable outbursts of negativity.

Cyrus managed to garner most of the kudos for the successful progress on the new software, deciding not to draw attention to Nathan's heroic journey into the unknown. His explanation being that the top brass might not have sanctioned the radical use of a human brain. Sal Goering let the suggestion pass. He knew who had overcome the problems and he was content. He needed people like Cyrus in the organisation.

CHAPTER 4

The metal detector, a limousine of a machine, with none of the mechanical ignorance of the operator, suddenly shrilled in the chill Yorkshire morning. Nathan, started abruptly, then realising it was his kit which was chirruping, tried to adjust the controls on the handgrip without dropping it. He fumbled until he chanced on turning a knob in the right direction and the alert of the shrieking "Trove-Seeker Mk 2" sank to a buzz. His immediate reaction was that he was no more capable with this lump of electronic hardware than he had been with a double barrelled Springfield. Although, at least, he seemed to have scored a hit.

It was a year since he had withdrawn from the shooting syndicate to get himself into a social activity that better suited his personality. Metal detecting seemed to tick most of the boxes - outdoor activity, an element of adventure and new faces.

The hum of the detector rose and fell as he manoeuvred it from side to side in a passable imitation of the metronomic style so natural to others in the party. To Nathan's inexperienced ear, the tonal pitch of the "audio discriminator" meant little. He checked the LCD screen but it didn't help. The "visual target identification" jumped back and forth between ferrous and non-ferrous, apparently unable to make up its mind. Perplexed but revelling in his outing with the "Friends of the Fields", he found it easy to appear more competent than he actually was.

He checked the automatic ground setting was correctly identifying fast draining sandy soil, ruling out the possibility of a false signal. Then, without looking up, he called out to the middle aged woman in the pink anorak who, 30 yards away, was nearest to him in the line: "Doris," and pointing to the find, "probably another buckle." Doris gave him a thin smile and continued her own sweep. It was a clue to his inexperience with women that he had hoped to meet ladies of his own age when he joined the metal detecting club - preferably younger and shapelier than Doris. More like the alluring redhead he had encountered on his successful American consultancy. Though if it was romance he was seeking, he was now looking in the wrong place. At least, he thought, the ladies he had encountered through field sport had had something to say for themselves, even if they had shown no interest in the shy and famously poor shot.

A collection of artefacts recovered from the field was already covering the tarpaulin pegged out on the margin of the land. Each item was labelled with the finder's name, map reference, time and date. There were lengths of rusted metal, which had been provisionally identified as parts of spurs, incomplete horseshoes, musket balls and a small filigreed plate, thought to be the base of a scabbard. Several corroded baldricks, or buckles, and some rusted scraps that at one time might have been metal buttons were also there. None of these discoveries caused him any surprise. They were only to be expected on Towton Moor, where, on Palm Sunday in March 1461, a Yorkist army, mustered by Edward 1V, overcame Henry V1's superior force of 20,000 to 30,000 supporters of the House of Lancaster. Nathan knew it was generally accepted to be the bloodiest engagement ever fought on English soil. The dead were said to number around 28,000. Both sides had given no quarter and were known to have butchered prisoners and the wounded. Lancastrian survivors of the battle, who had fled the field for sanctuary at York, were pursued mercilessly. Those who made it to lie in the narrow streets of the city, were either given a quick trial and then executed – or slain where they lay. Such behaviour had become common during the later battles of the Wars of the Roses. It had been widely reported recently that, in a dig in the grounds of Towton Hall, archaeologists had excavated a grave containing twenty six skeletons. A keen amateur historian in the metal detecting club had assured everyone: "Significantly, none was wearing a helmet. They had been executed after the battle, each with as many as ten fierce blows to the head... so much for chivalry!"

Permission to sweep the site had been readily granted by the landowner, who had lately suffered unwelcome visits from so-called 'Nighthawks', unauthorised detectors who "vacuumed up" anything interesting and sold it on the Internet. Important archaeological evidence was consequently lost.

Nathan's decision to take up detecting had been accelerated by the news media. An enthusiast in the East Riding of Yorkshire had unearthed a hoard of gold coins dating from the Roman period and had been photographed with the farmer who owned the land. Coincidentally, Nathan felt he had reached a point in life where he could enjoy learning something of the lifestyles of his ancestors. He had never had time to study history although it had always been of interest to him. He needed something more than television documentaries to fuel his interest. He was determined to bring a sparkle into his life, still with a desire to balance the stress of his career. The possibility that he might even discover buried treasure or some significant artefact would be a bonus. It certainly chimed better with his personality than shooting game birds did.

He took a quick peek around, checking the proximity and attitudes of other members of the party and saw them focussed on their own patches. He unslung a trenching tool from its back-pack – his own idea that – and gripping the shaft in his right hand, gave a couple of exploratory blows with the chisel end of the blade.

"Stop that... it might be an unexploded bomb, you dope!" The shout blasted across the moor and everyone looked his way.

"A bomb? Impossible! There was a crop in this field a month ago by the look of it. And not so much of the 'dope' if you don't mind," he yelled back.

"Of course it isn't a bomb, but you must treat every alert as though it is. That way you won't damage anything brought to the surface by cultivation."

The advice was followed by a patronising shake of the head. The speaker was a man, so prodigious in his success rate, that a collection of his discoveries occupied a complete display case with a brass plaque bearing his name in the Museum of Archaeology at nearby York. Mollified slightly, Nathan continued with his digging, sensing rather than feeling the steel blade of the trenching tool skirting around his find. As an earthworm wriggled back into a crevice created by his excavation, he spotted a wedge of contoured metal peeping through the soil. He tried the detector again. It confirmed his impression that the size of the object might cause a problem for one person getting it out of the ground. He puzzled how something so large could lie so close to the surface but remain undetected. He was pretty sure that the field had grown corn last summer. Why hadn't the blades of the plough fouled the buried object?

The find, which was beginning to appear under his efforts, seemed to be about the size of a sheep trough. Here and there, where Nathan's shovel work had been over enthusiastic, a metallic lustre glinted. Maybe a cannon or culverin, he thought, with a hint of rising excitement. No. It was more like...perhaps... a statue. A sculpture maybe? Or, if it were not so ridiculously unfeasible, a suit of armour? Intact after more than five centuries? Hardly! He slipped off the Barbour to give himself more freedom for the digging.

The first flakes of snow were so infrequent, Nathan failed to notice as, like aphids on a humid evening, they drifted silently across him.

Imperceptibly, they multiplied until a fine powder dusted the dig. He persevered, determined to explore the limits of his find, using his hands to brush away the gathering snowflakes. Bigger, fatter flakes, driven by a wind from the south, now intensified, developing into a solid blanket and blotting out treasure hunters only yards away. Head down and bent double, he laboured more frantically, obsessively sweeping aside the damp snow in an attempt to keep the object visible. He was totally unaware the others were packing up and hurrying towards their parked cars, eager to get out of the blizzard and begin their journey home before country lanes became blocked.

As she had passed him moments before, Doris, with the pink anorak, had voiced the collective decision to abandon work. She thought he had raised a hand in acknowledgement, but had reinforced the message as she had rushed by, shouting, "Let's get off this wretched moor before we're snowed in. We'll come back another time." Nathan's total absorption meant he heard none of this and Doris was soon invisible. She did not look back.

He was half aware now he was functioning on two different planes. His thoughts flashed back to the awful Battle of Towton and his heartbeat raced as blood-soaked images swamped his vision. It was accelerated by his hectic efforts to free the "find" from the grip of the land. Some unnatural compulsion compelled him to work even faster. His hands and arms operated robotically. Switching to the shovel to clear the steadily increasing covering of snow, his movements became mechanical, without conscious direction. His excitement overflowed and the sounds of battle swirled in his hearing as he lost himself to his task. Feeling ebbed from his hands. His movements became slower and less effective. Snow piled silently against him as he knelt beside his dig and as he finally sank forward to the ground, it gradually formed an immaculate shroud over his prone body.

CHAPTER 5

Thomas Courtenay, the 14th earl of Devon, eased sideways in the saddle and tried to relieve the pain in his right hip by forcing his left foot deeper into the stirrup. The manoeuvre worked for a short time until the mare caught a hoof on the frozen ground and stumbled. The Earl vented an agonised groan and reined his mount. Immediately, his Steward, a few paces behind, rushed forward.

"Fetch me a seat, Dogberry, or I shall end in the snow... and summon the surgeon. Should I not obtain relief soon, I shall lose my sanity."

He allowed himself to slip from the saddle, rather than dismount, knowing Dogberry would catch him as he collapsed from the horse's back. The wound had troubled him since the Battle of Wakefield three months earlier. Fighting on foot, he had taken a ferocious blow from a poleaxe, aimed at his shoulder but glancing down to his hip. His well fitting Italian armour prevented a mortal wound but the stroke had felled him. He was saved only by the intervention of his Men-at-Arms. Then, after two months recuperation on his estates in the South West, he had received the summons to join the king in the North and had called in his retainers and was now heading to support Henry. It would be another attempt to end the rivalries between the Houses of York and Lancaster with a set piece battle. There had been several in recent times but, on this occasion, there was a real prospect of resolution. The recently deposed Henry had drawn to his banner a massive army, including the most powerful families in the North. Most English nobility supported Henry and wished to restore the monarchy to the House of Lancaster. Nearly 30,000 loyalists had declared for the one they held to be the rightful monarch, despite Edward having gathered enough support for his own cause to have been proclaimed King in London earlier in the year. For his part, Edward was now gathering an army almost as big as that of Henry as he marched northwards. Adding to his host, he had also recruited mercenaries from England's lands in France. The Burgundians, especially, were skilled in the latest forms of warfare and, fighting in units armed with crude muskets as well as cannon, they made a formidable threat. Even more so at close quarters when they fired ball or steel bolts carrying arrowheads, which could pierce even the best armour. To these, they added another terror. Packing their culverins with wadding and dampened powder, they could discharge sheets of flaming hell, which they termed "wild-fire", into the enemy lines mere yards away.

Henry had his own artillery. He had emptied the Privy Wardrobe of the weaponry at the Tower of London, where it had been stored for the defence of the realm. Though having been collected over many years, largely on donations, much of it was outdated.

The Earl of Devon, in his 27th year, thought hard of the delicate balance of power held by the two aristocratic Houses as he awaited medical attention to arrive from the rear of the column. His surgeon had advised him not to lead his contingent or, alternatively, to make the journey by wagon. Although Devon wished to demonstrate his toughness and solidarity with Henry's cause and this would be achieved by sitting astride a war horse, leading his troops. Despite his wound having healed, there was still a great deal of swelling. The joint had been distorted and the bone fractured. He now walked with the aid of a crutch and riding involved acute discomfort. However, he felt he had to be seen to be leading his men if they were to arrive at the rendezvous in the right spirit for battle.

He looked back at the straggling line, which had drawn to a halt when he had dismounted. His 850 or so archers and infantry came because they lived and worked on his land and the pay he offered to go to battle was double that of their normal work as labourers, thatchers, ploughmen and foresters. There was also the prospect of pillage. These were not professional soldiers but peasant folk, obliged by Common Law to practice with their chosen weapons kept in their homes. They knew nothing of national politics and it hardly mattered to them who ruled England. The Feudal System was dying out but it was still customary to respond to their landlord's wishes. The Men-at-Arms, wealthier connections of the Earl, occupied posts in his household and administrative responsibilities on his estates. They were honour and duty bound. A handful of knights had also joined them, partly out of genuine respect for the Earl, who was expected to be made one of the commanders of Henry's army, but largely for the rewards and favours which would inevitably be passed down to the victors from a grateful king.

The portcullis was down at Micklegate Bar when Devon and his exhausted followers finally reached the fortified City of York, where Henry had chosen to base his army. Their progress to gain the city had been hampered by the thousands of men spread out in the surrounding forestry and farmland, most without cover of any description, fully exposed to the wintry weather. It was two days before Palm Sunday and, in that early Spring, it was cold and wet. It was a damp black evening, witheringly cold. In the open, braziers projected flickering images on the battlements and torches burned alongside the fortified gate. The banners of Devon were quickly recognised and cheering broke out from the walls, to be picked up by the masses camping in the woods nearby. Knights and Men-at-Arms were allowed into the city when the portcullis was raised. It was immediately lowered once they had passed through. The archers and infantrymen had to move south around the city walls, seeking shelter from the elements. Many thousands already camped, the luckier ones having brought pack horses carrying food, blankets and tents. Though most had to seek protection in the woods, where they scavenged fuel for fires and slept in the open. Smoke clung stubbornly to the wet ground and, where a fire had been well fuelled, coiled in the damp air.

Leaning heavily on his crutch, with Dogberry supporting his free arm, the Earl of Devon made way slowly to the castle, where Henry and Queen Margaret and their son, the Prince of Wales, were quartered. The narrow streets and inns were crowded with armed men, arguing in French and varieties of regional English, where the forthcoming conflict might take place. York's taverners and bakers worked non-stop, taking advantage of the occupation of the city. The sour tang of ale mixed with the delicious aromas of roasting pork and hot pies drifting from the doorways. Dogberry inhaled longingly and suggested that the Earl should stop for supper. However, Devon would not wait to pay his respects to the man he regarded as King. Overheard snatches of conversation suggested that most of the army hoped Edward would choose to attack the city. Though in their hearts, they knew that a decisive encounter would probably come on the Vale of York, where the open ground suited a pitched battle between the two gigantic armies.

Devon fretted for over two hours before being allocated quarters by Henry's Chamberlain. Then he went to reassert his allegiance. He left his crutch with Dogberry as he entered the Royal Chamber. It was poor accommodation but, fortunately, Henry had never been keen on splendour or ceremony. Devon was mildly surprised that Henry was accompanied by his wife. She stood to the former monarch's right hand but slightly forward of him. After formal greetings, it was Margaret who spoke first.

"You may address yourself to me, my Lord. I have the king's full authority to represent him."

Devon was taken aback. He had known Henry for several years and was usually addressed by his given name of Thomas. Devon's face was racked with pain and the agony in his hip caused his speech to see-saw wildly in volume. Margaret received the Earl's oath without any show of feeling, perhaps because she had received so many similar promises over the past few weeks.

Devon noted that the relationship between Margaret and Henry had changed radically since his last meeting with them. Margaret now maintained the familiar justifications of their claims, using similar vocabulary, but screwed up her eyes and frequently turned her head to glance at her husband. After his wounding at Wakefield, Devon had not fought at the subsequent clash at St Albans, where the Yorkists had been soundly beaten. Yet the story of how the King, laughing and occasionally breaking into song, sat beneath a tree to observe the battle, had been widely circulated at Court. Queen Margaret was said to have commanded the troops that day and had claimed victory.

"Will the battle come soon your majesty?" Devon asked hoarsely. Before Henry could think to reply, Margaret responded, showing she had completely taken over military command from her husband and was well briefed.

"We have scourers out and we are getting reliable information. Edward's army is closing from the South. He seeks to cross the Aire at Ferrybridge but we have deployed to deny him and have ordered demolition of the bridge. A confrontation will ensure soon. The armies are already under provisioned. Most of our men have not eaten these two days, except for what game they have caught or livestock they have stolen. The resolution of this matter cannot be long delayed."

Henry slowly turned to face Devon, smiling vacantly at his old ally before speaking in a quavering voice, for the first time: "I am glad you have come Thomas. I do so value your loyalty." He paused, apparently unsure of how to continue before finally adding, "Should we prevail, I shall return to London. Otherwise, we intend to move North to join my allies. We may continue to Scotland for sanctuary with friends of the Queen."

Surprised by this acceptance of the possibility of the defeat of his huge army, which Devon took to show lack of resolve, he was too much in pain to extend the audience. He bowed to the Queen without disclosing what was in his mind and simply asked to be excused, dragging himself off to his chamber with Dogberry, ignored, at his side.

That night, he was further troubled by his hip. The long journey to the North had jarred the misaligned fracture. Pain seared through him without respite. By morning, he was unable to leave his bed. Dogberry summoned one of the surgeons, who had failed to attend the night before, despite a promise from the Royal Chamberlain. Now the surgeon administered a herbal sedative and declared that it would be impossible for the Earl to take part in the forthcoming battle. He would be incapable of holding his seat on the journey to the battleground and, even were he to reach it; he would be unable to fight on foot, which would be expected of all the knights. In any case, he argued, the army was so large that the absence of one knight would make little difference to the outcome. Devon made a desperate attempt to swing his legs off the bed and to try to stand. The pain was too much and he collapsed unceremoniously halfway off the bed.

CHAPTER 6

On the eve of Palm Sunday, the vast army of the House of Lancaster mustered before the walls of York, flying the pennants and standards indicating their allegiances. In great confusion, due to their huge numbers and the wide variety of languages and dialects, they eventually formed up behind Henry's appointed Commander in Chief, Henry Beaufort 3rd Duke of Somerset. In great clamour with heralds and sergeants at arms contesting to pass on commands, they finally began their march south. At Tadcaster, some six miles distant, they learned from their scouts that, denied passage by the demolition of the bridge over the River at Ferrybridge, Edward had sent troops to ford the Aire a few miles away at Castleford. This manoeuvre being successful, they had encircled, ambushed and routed the smaller force of the House of Lancaster at Ferrybridge. The entire Yorkist army had then crossed the river unimpeded. Now they were reforming into battle groups under their leaders and continuing their march towards York.

Somerset received the devastating news calmly. A survivor of many battles in his military career, he knew that his next move was to select ground to give best advantage to his army. He took his time in choosing a plateau eight miles from York, close to the villages of Towton and Saxton. He then instructed his commanders to set about drawing up their troops in a line stretching almost a mile in width. The next day, on Palm Sunday 1461, the armies got their first sight of each other.

From York, a small detachment of mounted men wearing Henry's livery and led by a lightly armoured knight, had made its way forward across broken country. The detachment kept pace with the Somerset's leading troops but about a mile to their flank. The riders reached an elevated part of the vale, overlooking a moor and within the fringes of a wooded hillock, which provided good cover. They were in an excellent position to observe the gradual deployment of Henry's army along a front line of nearly a mile in length. Satisfied that this was the chosen ground for the forthcoming battle, the knight, a trusted member of Henry's household, found himself a seat on a fallen tree, and watched and waited. He had been entrusted by Margaret of Anjou with a special mission. As a snowstorm broke over the countryside, sweeping across the horizon from the south, he saw the two armies ranged against each other roughly 300 yards apart. As the armies appeared to pause in confrontation, the watcher saw the weather worsen. Snow began to blow in near horizontal fashion into the faces of Henry's archers, who vanished in the blizzard. At that point, Edward's archers were seen to move forward a further 100 paces, from where they launched a lethal and accurate barrage of armour piercing arrows.

CHAPTER 7

The hillside was churned into muddy sculptures, frozen into stone. An electric storm exploded between his ears when he tried to roll onto his side. Something sharp ripped his nose as he turned his head and his efforts to ease the cramp in his legs wrenched an animal gurgle from his throat. He was freezing. Nathan knew he was going to die. He wanted it to happen immediately.

Yet the torture persisted. Spread-eagled and face down in shallow snow, hurting in every centimetre of his body, he prised open an eyelid. Bewildered, his mind refused to process what he saw. He was surrounded by grotesque nightmares. Visibility was poor and falling snow imposed a theatrical dimension to the horror. However, there was no doubt. Hundreds of savages battered and lunged at each other in slow motion, their lead-weighted poleaxes and war-hammers clanging against armour. An unearthly cacophony bludgeoned his eardrums as, utterly terrified, he watched the violence. Surely, he had arrived in hell.

Ten metres away, someone in the chain mail and helmet of a mediaeval soldier stood over a fallen foe, systematically raising a weighted mace and bringing it crashing down. The blows were aimed at the visor and joints in the man's armour. When the assailant was satisfied, he took out a long dagger, knelt, and thrust it clinically through the gaps in the armour. Then he twisted it as his victim screamed. There was no mercy this day. The victor rose, panting, and slowly turned his head to Nathan, trapped beneath the twitching corpse of a horse.

"I'm not in the battle," Nathan blurted out in panic, "I'm not a soldier."

The man, short and heavy, with a small round head and misshapen face, stumped slowly towards him, his mace swinging menacingly by his side. He stood over the prostrate figure and saw he had no weapons nor armour and wore no Household colours. It saved Nathan's life. The soldier called to two men enthusiastically robbing a corpse, one of many on the surrounding ground.

"Goodrich, Calvert, come see this one." The men, one tall and clad in an assortment of ill-fitting armour, and the other, shorter but with the powerful upper body of an archer, finished removing the dead man's boots. Then the older of the two ordered, "Hold hard, Negus. Let me look." He strode over and studied Nathan with steely eyes, "He's not wounded but the horse is dead, or soon will be." The fat one raised his mace above his head: "Shall I do him?"

Goodrich, who appeared to be of senior rank, gestured Negus to lower the mace and drew a huge and bloody sword, which he held against Nathan's neck. He raised his helmet and his voice was coarse and loud enough to be heard above the maelstrom. Blood mixed with spittle as he spat out his question, "For whom have ye come? Why wear ye no colours?" His heavy accent made it hard to understand.

Unable to rationally cope with his situation, Nathan eventually began to realise that the reason he was unable to move was that he was trapped under a dead horse... His legs and the lower part of him were pinned to the ground. His mind began to clear and he shouted, "I'm a doctor, I can bandage your wounds." The soldiers stared at him, uncomprehending. Eventually, Goodrich seemed to understand: "Bind wounds, do you? Then ye should be with the baggage train."

Negus interrupted: "I should kill him. The order was 'no quarter' to be given or accepted, and that from the King." The bloodthirsty little man dangled his mace inches from Nathan's head.

The leader of the trio defused the stand-off with his decision: "And you, Negus, have killed your share this day. We will not do one of our own. Let him tend our wounds. If he lies, we can finish him then. Come, see if we can move the horse."

The three, displaying tremendous strength, took hold of one of the hind legs and, bit by bit, dragged the beast far enough for Nathan to wriggle free. He lurched to his feet but immediately fell, dizzy and numb. He tried again, staggering into the archer, whom he now realised was a youth, possibly in his late teens. The lad, Calvert, supported him while he regained the circulation in his legs.

Nathan stared at the man whom he had watched despatch an enemy so pitilessly. Negus, probably back in some previous combat, had taken a fearful blow to his face. It had left a gruesome dent in his forehead, smashed his cheekbone and left him with one eye lower than the other. A fresh wound started above his eye and ran diagonally down his face. He had other injuries and blood soaked through his long chain mail vest, which was ripped in parts. It also dripped from his left hand. Nathan seized his opportunity. "Let me help you," he pleaded, miming applying a bandage to clarify his intent. The noise and the raw wind made it hard to make himself heard.

Nathan borrowed a dagger and cut the heraldic livery from the dead horse. Using snow to clean the ugly one's wounds, he bandaged them as tightly as he was able. The stink of the man, the smell of him beneath the armour and his unshaven, blood encrusted face, was repulsive. Laughter broke the tension as Goodrich and Calvert teased Negus for his odd appearance with flamboyant strips of red and gold tapestry from the horse concealing half his face.

"You look like a right jolly blacksmith," joked Calvert, "horse blanket for a horse doctor," and then laughed hugely at his simple jibe. Negus, who ran the village forge when he wasn't being paid to fight, flexed one massive forearm and raised the mace in mock threat.

"You can try a taste of my medicine if you wish, boy," he countered.

Nathan, astonished that they could banter in this setting, was now simultaneously acclimatising to his odd surroundings and racking his brain as to how he came to be in this place. It was an insoluble puzzle and he had to keep his mind focussed on staying alive. He took courage to ask where they came from and this began an uneven conversation with both parties struggling to understand each other. Although there were corpses in near proximity, the nearest combatants were some distance from them. Nathan eventually made out that he and his companions came from Shropshire, where Goodrich worked as a thatcher and Calvert was champion archer of the village. He could draw a bow with pull strength of 150 lb, he bragged, and put up to ten arrows in the air within a minute.

"I shot all my arrows and many of their's fell short. Now, I fight with a sword," he said, when asked where his bow was. Noting the lad's warlike demeanour, Nathan had no doubt how well he would acquit himself. He was about to ask more penetrating questions when, out of the mist and light snow, a large unit of soldiers in strange uniforms and carrying heavy weaponry marched towards them. Goodrich grabbed hold of his vest with the Yorkist colours and raised his sword as he shouted something in a language Nathan failed to understand. The soldiers raised their own pennants and stopped in front of Goodrich.

After a brief exchange of words with much gesturing and hand signals, Goodrich shook the hand of one of the men and turned to face his own group.

"They are Burgundian mercenaries," he explained, "but not much use to us today. Their gunpowder has been soddened by the snow and they are more in danger of blowing themselves up rather than the enemy. They are retreating behind our lines, probably hoping to find dry powder."

Negus snorted his disgust as the Burgundians trouped past him away from the battle.

"I made bolts and balls for their culverins before we left home. I expected them to blow holes in the Lancastrian lines to save our skins. But they're getting money for nothing," he complained.

Nathan watched the mercenaries march off and then felt it was the right time to find out more about his new allies. Struggling to understand each others' questions and answers, they told him they were part of the contingent of a wealthy family on whose land they lived. Negus, a feared foot soldier, was involved in his fourth campaign, while Goodrich had survived battles twice before. As an archer, Calvert was earning four times his farm labourer's wage. They had followed their landowner to the battle not only to claim soldier's wages, but also to enrich themselves with plunder.

When he judged he had ingratiated himself a little, Nathan summoned the courage to ask about the armies engaged in the battle. Before he could quiz them, the light hearted mood abruptly changed as a hostile group emerged from the mist and headed towards them, apparently weighing up the odds. The noise of two great armies had muffled their approach, even though the battle had now broken into scores of confused melees. The men wore different colours to Goodrich's little band and he shouted a warning, "Shall we run or fight, there's five of 'em?" Calvert's answer was to wave his sword above his head and run at the men, screeching, "Edward and York". Goodrich and Negus immediately joined in, the little fat man moving at surprising speed over the rough ground and both yelling the battle cry. Nathan was petrified. Clad in anorak and trekking trousers, he had no armour or weapon, and no wish to fight. He was sick with fear. Yet the war cry gave him a clue to what had befallen him.

As the groups clashed, the athletic young archer suddenly squatted and swung a fearsome blow with his sword at the leader's legs. The man realised too late Calvert's purpose and took the full force. He went down, cleaved through the knees. Calvert jumped over him and engaged a second man who, unable to match his opponent in skill or power, turned and ran. Negus, a fearsome sight with the bandaged head, swung the mace high and charged the tallest who poked out his blade. Negus lowered the arc of his swing so the chain wound twice around the extended sword, and yanked it from his grasp. However, the Lancastrian held a dagger in his other hand and lunged at his great belly. The mail tunic saved his life but Negus gasped as a rib bent under the force of the blow. He smashed the shaft of the mace hard into the opponent's face and was about to swing again when Calvert chopped the man's knees from behind. Negus then flailed him until he lay still.

Nathan stood transfixed. Then, fired by the adrenalin of fear and caught up in the desperation of fighting, he snatched up a bill with a broken shaft.

The point of the bill was long and sharp and a wide axe blade protruded from lower down the shaft. The skirmish and the noise and fury of the danger stoked his self-preservation and he shouted and threatened the enemy with his weapon. Goodrich was engaged in feints and a stand-off with his chosen adversary. When he noticed Nathan, he shouted, "Behind them," and Nathan saw the advantage. Whilst Goodrich kept the attention of the Lancastrian, Nathan circled behind and thrust the point of the bill with all his strength into the man's back. His victim wore no mail and his breastplate protected only his front. The point went five inches into flesh and the victim threw back his elbows, bellowing. When he went to ground, Goodrich slashed his throat.

Nathan dropped the pike and stared down at the mortally wounded man. This was a human being. Emotion surged up. The ability to move, to say something – anything – left him. He was paralysed with guilt and shivering madly. Then he vomited.

The fifth man turned to run but was engaged by Calvert and Negus and battered to the ground to become another victim of the dagger. After Calvert despatched the wounded, Goodrich checked their clothes and possessions. One of them wore a medallion, which appeared to be gold, and Goodrich broke the chain and stuffed the trophy inside his tunic.

Goodrich stared at Nathan, still traumatised with what he had done: "Take any armour you can and their boots. One over there wears a brigandine lined with iron plate. It didn't save him but it's better than your dress." When Nathan made no move, Goodrich shouted into his face, "Make a move man or you'll die on this field." Nathan vomited again and felt numb but was able to comprehend what he had to do.

Glad of the extra clothing, he slowly donned the heavy tunic then watched Goodrich scour the field and return with a tattered bib, on which were crudely painted the colours of a Yorkist general. "Put this on and all will know where your loyalties lie."

No more than half an hour had passed since the skirmish and the search for armour, but the line of battle had receded further and the sound of the fray came only in muffled bursts. Goodrich stared into the mist, "The Lancastrians show their arses. They're leaving the field. We can pursue or go back to the baggage train and see if any victuals have arrived."

***

For the past three days, none of them had eaten anything apart from raw turnips, uprooted from the fields as they marched. Edward had forbidden foraging on pain of death. Now Negus snorted and wiped a grubby arm across his nose: "We shall find no pickings in the baggage train. I am for pursuit until we have our pokes full. Then we can fill our bellies." His passion swayed young Calvert and the party moved forward over thawing ground, stepping around corpses of both sides, stopping only to relieve the dead and dying of their jewellery. Once they reached the horizon, where the army of the House of Lancaster had been drawn up at the start of the day, the hill sloped steeply to a narrow river, swollen with melting snow.

Indefinable foreboding rose in Nathan's chest. He had a premonition of horror and had to force his legs to carry him. "Come on," Calvert urged, noticing his reluctance, adding "and remember, no quarter."

As they ran down the slope, a wall of shouts and screams rose from the river banks. Drawing closer, Nathan's fears were realised. Where a ford had existed before the river flooded, a huge crush of the enemy was attempting to wade across. Encumbered by their armour but forced along by the weight of the masses trying to flee, many lost their footing and sank below the surface to be trampled into a ghastly bridge of bodies. With pikes and axes, the rampant Yorkists hacked at the backs of the fleeing throng, adding panic to their flight. Some Lancastrians threw off their armour and tried to swim across but were swept away. Downstream, the shallow river ran crimson.

Nathan felt he was about to faint. He had heard this story of the slaughter of the retreating force at the River Cock from a fellow treasure hunter during their survey of Towton Moor. With a scrambled brain, he stood in a waking trance. The rout continued for more than an hour before Goodrich pulled back, exhausted but elated. In high spirits and brandishing trophies stripped from the enemy, they began the uphill walk to the baggage train behind their lines.

"How are you called, friend?" asked Goodrich after a while, as they trudged over the icy moorland.

"I was Christened Nathanial but I go by Nathan," he replied and wondered what sick twist of fate landed him in the middle of the bloodiest battle ever fought on English soil.

CHAPTER 8

The seven year-old sobbed so piteously that his mother, Queen of all England until a few months before, motioned to the nursemaid to bring the child to her bed. The words she whispered in comfort were French but she raised her eyes to engage those of the nurse as she promised the boy, "Shout your defiance little one, you will 'ere be king of this troubled land."

Their room in the Castle at York was hardly appropriate for royalty. Set in the residential part of the keep and considered to be the safest place to be during any siege, it was sparsely provided with furniture. A single fireplace, the walls devoid of tapestries or paintings to soften the stone and a large bed which cried out for the attention of a skilled French carpenter. Her husband's chamber close by was little better, but two fires burning constantly meant it was warmer for the semi-invalid she still referred to as the King.

Ah, the King, she thought. What a snivelling defeatist he had become. Unable to walk any distance, confused and incapable of making decisions. An apology for a monarch. No longer the proud nobleman who wooed her from the age of fifteen. Margaret of Anjou, eight years younger than her husband, had come to the conclusion she had to do more than support the wreck he had become. She must take over Government and secure the succession for her son, the Prince of Wales. The rule of the self-proclaimed Edward 1V must be brief.

Even before the age of 15, Margaret had begun to show her strong will. She was not typical of the pampered offspring of French gentry and was quite prepared to demonstrate her enterprise and self confidence. When her Latin tutor at the Abbey of Jonquille falsely told her father that his daughter did not study hard enough, she avenged herself by locking him in his pantry, where he remained for three days before being released, stinking and subdued.

Despite many titles, her father was not a wealthy man and Margaret learnt that a favourable marriage would be essential if she was to enjoy the status her titles gave her. She was an alluring girl, well favoured by nature, tall, with flawless features. She needed no schooling to ensure the Earl of Suffolk sent to vet her as a possible wife for Henry V1, returned to England impressed. Later, when it came time to leave home for her betrothal, she sold her jewellery so that she could hire attendants rather than appear for the ceremony without means.

Now, Henry's fragile mental condition had collapsed. When he was not incubated in melancholia, he was at prayer or in the company of religious teachers. He was incapable of dealing with the clamouring English nobility, plotting to advance selfish interests in a Court that deteriorated daily. When Margaret's son, Edward, the Prince of Wales, had been born, conjecture flourished. When he saw the child for the first time, Henry was said to have declared the boy was "the son of the Holy Spirit".

As the plotting and manoeuvring intensified, Margaret played an ever-growing role in Government and had not drawn back from the prospect of civil war. The whole of the North of England supported her, together with the Scots. She could not foresee the terrible end her army would meet on the windswept contours of a Yorkshire moor. Today, with her husband cringing in the next room, she fretted whilst the set piece battle reached its gory finale.

A frantic clamour erupted outside the bed chamber and, before the maid could get to it, the door was flung wide and a messenger fell into the room. "Oh your majesty, the news is bad. There has been a great battle. We have been defeated and you must flee with the King and the Prince."

Margaret studied the messenger. She said nothing. Then, her face grim, she cursed the news, "Flee? How can you be sure? Edward does not have enough troops to defeat my 30,000!"

The young man, conscious of his orders, declined to argue, "I go to rouse the King your majesty. You must dress for a long and hard journey." He backed hastily to the door where, half way through a clumsy bow, he turned and fled.

Within the hour, Margaret was seated in an enclosed carriage with Henry, who was immune to what was happening around him. The Prince of Wales, swathed in lambskins, was clutched to his mother's bosom as the cumbersome vehicle bounced its way through the city gates and headed north. At the same time, an empty decoy wagon painted in the Royal colours and flying Henry's standard, raced out of the east gates of the city with a troop of horsemen blowing their horns in full fanfare.

Every jolt from the iron clad wheels reminded Margaret of her vulnerability. She was familiar with adversity since her marriage was intended to end the wars between France and England. Her husband had not bothered to visit France for the betrothal, sending the Earl of Suffolk to represent him. It was the start of an unhappy arrangement, which hardened Margaret to her role as an unpopular Queen. Not only was she young and inexperienced, she was French in a country which had been at war with her homeland for generations. She had not visited France since her departure, whilst her cousin had become king.

"Horseback would have been quicker and made our escape more certain," she admonished Henry, "The prince could have ridden pillion with one of the guards." He did not reply but stared blankly at the richly upholstered interior of the carriage. Tears ran slowly down his pale face. The spirited young wife made her decision: "My Lord, I think it would be best if I did not stay with you in the coming months whilst we rebuild our armies. I shall take the prince and sail for France to entreat the King. Shall I offer to give back Calais if he will agree to help?"

Still, Henry did not speak, bowing his head and retreating to a place no one could reach.

She drew back the curtain from the hole which served as a window. A dozen knights, flying no banners and fully cloaked to conceal the Royal insignia on their tunics, rode with the carriage, a meagre guard for a one time king and queen. Margaret looked carefully at the riders until she spotted the broad shouldered figure she had hoped to see, at the front of the troop. The knight saw her looking and touched his lips with his right fist. She felt safer then. Yet there was no pursuit. The weather had improved, the snow had stopped and the party made good speed to Boroughbridge. Once across the Ure, they settled at a less reckless pace.

A day later, with Royal pennants now held high, they reached the lands of powerful friends, the Percy family, safe from the vengeance the victors of Towton were taking on all who had opposed them.

CHAPTER 9

"You are the Earl of Devon, are you not?" Three armed men stood round the bed as one of them addressed its occupant, bending over him to identify his face. Bewildered by the rough wakening, the Earl stared around him before finally replying, "I have that honour, sir. And who are you?"

The man returned a hostile stare and continued without disclosing his own identity. "His Majesty, Edward, King of England, will arrive in the city tonight and I am charged to seize all who supported Henry of Lancaster in treasonable opposition."

"I am no traitor, sir. How can it be treason when Henry wore the crown? I supported him as my duty. If Edward is now truly King, let him send for me and I will have no conscience to go against him. I uphold the institution of the Crown, not the individual." Devon's reply drew no acknowledgement and the inquisitor turned his attention to Dogberry, who was peering around the door that he had recently opened to admit the visitors.

"Get your master from his bed and dress him. Then bring him to the Great Hall and deliver him to me," he ordered.

"I fear he is unable to walk today, my lord. May he join you in the hall on the morrow?" the Steward asked, naively.

"No, you oaf. He will not be joining us to sup. He is to answer questions from the court. Not able to walk? Then carry him. I heard we nearly had him at Northampton. This time he will not escape justice."

In the Great Hall of York Castle, tables had been arranged to form a half circle of seating with a large clear space in the centre. This space was now occupied by some of Edward's high ranking followers. To the side, were leading citizens of the city, assembled to witness and, no doubt, be intimidated by what they would hear and see. The Earl of Devon leaned heavily on his crutch as he was asked how many troops he had contributed to Henry's army. The question, put without preamble, took him by surprise. He had expected to be quizzed on the nature of the oath of allegiance he had taken years ago, or matters concerning Henry's current whereabouts and intentions. The simple request for the numbers of his supporters took him off guard.

"There are some 850 of my tenants, fifty or more of my Household and eight members of my family," he stated.

"You mean there once were these numbers. They are all dead on Towton's fields where you sent them." The finality of the statement was dreadful. "You are guilty and you do not deny it. Taking arms against the King is treason, as you must know. Take him out and remove his rebellious head," the interrogator paused before adding, "and display it at Traitor's Gate with the others."

The Earl tried to speak, to argue his position and that of the court, but shouts emanating from the audience drowned his attempts. As guards grabbed him, he stoically squared his shoulders and braced himself to die with dignity in the manner of true nobility. He was dragged, limping, from the Castle into the Market Place and forced to kneel with his outstretched arms supporting his shoulders parallel to the ground. Senior burgesses and elders of York, still fearful that they might be called to account for harbouring Henry and his supporters before the battle, were made to stand in a half-circle to witness the execution. There being no block, the decapitation was performed with an already bloody sword and several strikes were necessary before the head was severed. Taking the gruesome exhibit by the hair and raising it aloft, a soldier then paraded it along the road to Micklegate Bar, now so called " Traitors' Gate", where it was passed up to another guard on the parapet. This man was lowered by rope a few feet down the battlements to impale the head on a metal spike. Until recently, the same spike had borne the head of Edward's own father, brought to York after capture at Wakefield. Now it displayed the heads of some of those responsible for his death.

CHAPTER 10

Cyrus Goldbeam nudged the lever of the Jaguar's automatic drive and flicked the switch to "W" for better traction control. He loved the automobile, the symbol of his status in the corporation. A top-of-the-range 3.5 litre saloon in metallic maroon was a statement of his personality. Fast, distinctive and difficult to ignore. There was a forecast for worsening weather but he figured with the Jag's traction control unit and the winter tyres working in tandem, he could press on.

The Texan allowed himself a quick gloat and, as he often did, congratulated himself on his achievement that day. It had meant an early plane to Boston for the meeting and not absolutely everything had gone to plan. However, overall, he felt he could indulge in celebration. "A win for you, Cyrus and the finger to Sal Goering," he said aloud. He had organised a secret meeting with the head of arch-rivals, Scaife Sciences Inc, and had sold Bagnold down the river. His reward for this betrayal: a million and a half bucks in a Cayman Island bank. He would carry on with Bagnold for a year or so, feigning dismay at the way the competition had seized a share of the market. Then he could drift away or, better still, get himself made redundant with a golden handshake.

The luckiest part of his deceit was that he had stumbled across the knowledge that Scaife were working on an almost identical product but were at an early stage of development. He had been in the right place at the right time - a noisy strip joint in New York's Greenwich Village - when he had half recognised one member of a group two tables away. He had been intending to go over and join them but it had then dawned on him that the guy he knew was a top product development engineer from Scaife Sciences, their foremost competitors. One indiscreet conversation and maybe he could overhear something to his advantage.

In the clamour and catcalls of the striptease routines, it was easy to eavesdrop. The executive he had identified obviously did not know him and by standing with his back to the group, he could hear most of what they said without being noticed. He was not disappointed. One of them was complaining to the others that Scaife could never hope to crack their problems on the neuro-surgical package because of a reluctance to bring in people with enough clout.

Chewing over this information later, Cy had first had every intention of reporting to his board that Scaife were trying to penetrate the neurosurgical market sector in which Bagnold held the lead. Yet then it occurred to him that he may be able to devise a plan to benefit himself rather more than his employers.

Finding out where Scaife were held up and then selling them the plans meant that they would be on equal terms with Bagnold without laying out \$3.75m in R and D costs. As he mused on his luck and cleverness, the wipers cut in to clear the first hints of weather on the windscreen. Soon, the forward view was a kaleidoscope of giant flakes and, within minutes, the road had disappeared under a seamless white blanket. Snug in the cockpit of the Jag, Cy wallowed in the knowledge he had got one over on Sal, who always took the credit for Bagnold's sale successes.

"Up yours, Sal," he said, addressing the burr walnut dash, "and up yours too, you smart-ass Limey Joker." Cy's dislike of Nathan underlined his own insecurity. In a business where technical genius ruled, Cyrus was a citizen 2nd Class, even as sales supremo. That Brit had got right under his skin. It wasn't so much the man's talent he found irritating, it was his easy way with words and the manner in which he could dismantle a contrary argument, leaving his adversary looking foolish.

Nathan Chalmers, whose name Cy was pleased to pronounce "Chal – mus", had been introduced to the neuro-surgical project at International Vice President level by Sal. So he had not had to fight his way through the layers of management Cyrus had negotiated in 14 years with the company. The Limey had not only gained a reputation as a genius, he also won the affections of Meg St Clair, the ornamental head girl in Marketing Services. The statuesque Meg was a woman on whom Cyrus had his own designs for those away weekends at sales conferences. Well, the dickhead would have something new to worry about soon. When Scaife announced its launch, Sal might be encouraged to harbour a suspicion on how they managed it and the false clues Cyrus would scatter would lead him to suspect his grouse shooting buddy, sufficiently to give him the Big "E".

Yes, Cyrus felt pretty damn good with his day's work. He kept an eye on his speed, allowing the heavy saloon to cruise around the middle forties, fast enough in these conditions. There was hardly any other traffic on the road, one or two trucks, taking it easy like himself. As he put the Jaguar into a long right hand curve, he noticed a quarter of a mile ahead, the flare of two large headlights being joined alongside a second pair. What the hell, he thought, and it was a few seconds before he realised what was happening. One slower truck was being overtaken by another and they were headed for him. Cyrus swung the wheel to make an acute right turn off the highway onto the shoulder, and simultaneously floored the brake pedal. The effect was to make the Jag skid on in a straight line, broadside to the oncoming collision. The truck tried to steer away from the impact, but it was impossible. It smashed the Jaguar amidships and drove it back 50 yards on the snowy surface in the direction of its travel.

When the police and ambulance arrived, Cyrus Goldbeam had been dead half an hour. Searching through the dead man's bloodied billfold, the patrolman withdrew a couple of business cards which identified the fatality. There was another item of interest which drew a gasp from the officer. A credit slip from an international bank in the Cayman Islands, confirming an electronic transfer of one and a half million dollars that very day.

CHAPTER 11

Over the bleak moorland, four exhausted warriors headed for the baggage train. Nathan did not feel that he was a prisoner although his relationship with the men was fragile, but he knew better than to run off, even had he been physically capable of it. Where would he run? Having witnessed the slaughter at the River Cock, he knew he was caught up in the battle of Towton. He also knew this took place on Palm Sunday in 1461. He was also aware that his presence there defied logic and all known science. It was impossible. Is this what madness felt like? The problem was too difficult, too complex. Then, an icy wind whipped needles of snow into his face and the reverie was obliterated.

The sound of fighting had long since faded as they approached the camp of the baggage train. When they drew nearer, Calvert, shielding his eyes from the wind, suddenly let out a curse, ran forward a few paces and then dropped into a crouch. They all stared into the blowing snow and what he saw made Nathan forget all about his own dilemma. Troops sporting the livery of the House of Lancaster, were riding down the boys in charge of the baggage. Nathan saw armoured men, some on foot, some mounted, laying about with sword and lance, striking down panicking servants and medical men.

Without warning, Goodrich grabbed Calvert and dragged him to the ground. "We are no match for mounted troops. Keep down until they ride off," he ordered. It lasted only a few minutes before the cavalry did indeed gallop away.

When Nathan and his group reached the train, the killers had melted into the low cloud. The camp had been wrecked. Dead and dying lay all around. Those able to do so, tried to stand and collect horses which had escaped the slaughter. Other mounts and mules lay kicking, disembowelled with the lance or slashed with the sword.

Calvert brandished his dagger in anger:"Those evil swine," he raged, "the grooms were unarmed. The followers of Lancaster now wage war on children."

Nathan knelt beside a dying boy and tried to stop blood running from a gash to the lad's head. "Get me some bandages, Calvert. Search the bags for anything which may be used as binding."

Calvert ransacked the bags strewn around the area and returned with shirts and tent material, which he cut into strips. Nathan used snow on the boy's wound to make the blood congeal. He wrapped a bandaged round the victim's head. He and Calvert dressed as many wounds as they could for the next hour. However, Nathan realised he needed to cauterize the more severe injuries. He was no doctor but he knew enough first aid gathered from his days in the Boy Scouts. He couldn't stand by and watch the injured bleed to death..

"Get that fire going again," he ordered and Calvert instantly accepted the role of servant and steadily revived the blaze. "Give me your knife," Nathan ordered and the boy handed over the long dagger which had tormented so much Lancastrian flesh this day. He watched as Nathan made the blade red hot before pressing it firmly over a deep wound on the chest of one of the young victims. The boy screamed and Negus and Goodrich moved forward and grabbed Nathan by the shoulders.

"They will die if I don't stop them losing blood. I must seal the wounds and hope they are strong enough to survive," he explained. He knew little of first aid but the desperate situation leant him inspiration and he went to work on a dozen of the victims. "We shall have to get them to shelter, somewhere safe and under cover," he told Calvert, who had been watching in fascination. To a peasant lad, it seemed a wizard was at work.

While Goodrich and Negus set about checking each prone figure for signs of life, and Nathan was occupied with bandaging those who might be saved, several knights flying the pennons of York, arrived to rest themselves and make sure the grooms had fed their horses. A few infantry from the rear guard had, that morning, been left to protect the baggage train from plundering by local villagers, but an attack in such force had not been envisaged. Aghast at the work of the Lancastrian cavalrymen, the knights managed to round up several horses which had scattered during the raid but many more had to be destroyed. The knights were about to move off when one of them singled out Nathan.

"You there," he began, "I have taken a wounding. Will you attend me? I will pay well for your skills."

"There is no need for payment," Nathan assured him, "Let me see your injury."

The knight had received a blow that had pierced his mail skirt and opened his thigh below the hip. It was an ugly cut and Nathan guessed it would have to be stitched. He said as much and explained that he had no means of carrying out the work. Though the knight ordered his men to search the baggage strewn amongst the bodies and instructed them what to look for. In a few minutes, they returned with a surgeon's bag, complete with opiates and herbs to dull pain and a range of crude surgical tools and thread. Nathan marvelled at the stoicism of his patient as, for the first time in his life, he stitched human flesh. He had had no training and relied upon memories of visits to the Casualty Department of the hospital in his boyhood. He recalled how cuts sustained from tumbles from his bike or from climbing trees had been expertly stitched by the doctors. It was not a neat job he did now but the drawing together of the edges of the cut was achieved and he felt that, if infection could be avoided, the wound would heal. He bound the wound with the most suitable piece of cloth he had.

The man, held out his hand, "I am Roger of Launceston. You will come with us. There are many of noble family lying in the village church that need your attention," he said, and he asked his name.

Nathan mumbled that he was from the North and added something about losing his leader. Then, realising he had received more of a command than a suggestion, he picked up the surgeon's bag. He told Calvert to collect what useful material he could and the two set off to follow the knights on foot, leaving Negus and Goodrich to guard the camp. Nathan called to them as he left, "When you have horses, bring the wounded to the church or they will die of exposure tonight." As he tramped after the knight, his thoughts returned again to the blind alley of extraordinary events which had brought him to this place and of the nightmare of Towton field.

CHAPTER 12

The church of St Michael was the focal point of Saxton village close by the battleground, an ancient stone built refuge with a Saxon tower. It was surrounded by a well populated cemetery, which would soon see more interments. Once beautifully bordered with elegant trees and yew hedges, the churchyard had been stripped to fuel fires, outside and inside the church. The alluring smell of cooking, together with the smoke and heat, somehow restored a sense of reality. Weary and wounded knights stretched out on the tombstones or used them as tables for a meal. A sarcophagus provided a solid table for six men-at-arms devouring hot food, prepared by a woman in nun's habit. To Nathan, it resembled nothing more so than the set of an historical film.

Inside, Nathan was met with a concerto of languages and dialects, which made it impossible to understand anything being said. The tones of Gascony and laborious Latin sentences clashed with the burrs of South West England and abrasive exchanges in what Nathan took to be Anglo Saxon. He noted that all tapestries and chalices, even the heavy ceremonial cross itself, had been hidden away and the altar stripped of its ornate cloth. Devoid of religious ornament, its bleak stone walls seemed well suited to the role of mortuary. Some of those who had withdrawn in sheer exhaustion from combat had found shelter by climbing into the bell tower. Their armour and weapons were stacked at the foot of the access ladder, watched over by a Steward, awaiting their return to combat.

The nave aisle resembled an abattoir. Priests, their vestments muddied to the waist and heavily blood stained, moved among the dying, absolving sins. Stripped of their armour, Nathan could see some of the stricken were badly mutilated. He could not imagine how they had got to the church. The bodies of some of high birth lay with dignity in the apse. He gasped as two nuns, straining to ease the armoured boot from a semi-conscious man of obvious wealth, were horrified to find the man's foot parted from his mangled leg. Astonishingly, no screams of pain escaped from the mutilated victim before he lay still and Nathan realised he must have fainted. All around, using the altar as a desk, Stewards were recording the names of the fallen. The corpses of those of lesser breeding had been carried outside and piled in a corner of the churchyard, where a second priest was commending their souls to God. More Stewards were engaged in the business of selecting suitable sites for mass graves, where the dead of both armies could be buried.

Pews had been commandeered as beds and operating tables. Anguished moans punctuated the air and, in a macabre counterpoint, in the main aisle, a minstrel played and sang ballads of bravery and battle. Nathan was staggered by the numbers of wounded, some already dying and others, freshly arrived, who would surely bleed to death. The surgeons here had followed the battle line closely as it moved in the action and had avoided the attack on the baggage. Now they were earning their retainers, trying to save lives with their primitive medicine. For many, Nathan noticed the only salve was egg yolk to stem bleeding or, for others, the red hot knife. There was little hygiene and no antiseptics, although he did see alcoholic drink being passed round. He received many strange looks when he motioned to the working surgeons that they should apply the alcohol to the wounds instead of it being drunk as a pain killer. When he tried a practical demonstration, the wounded man screamed abuse and tried to strike Nathan with piece of rope he had been biting to help him tolerate the pain.

Heads turned as Roger of Launceston rescued Nathan and guided him through the crowd to the vestry door flanked by guards wearing insignia of the House of York. They stepped aside and the knight knocked and entered. Inside, being stripped of his armour by his Steward, stood the 19 year-old King of England, excitedly in conversation with his Steward on choice of clothing, replacing his sweat soaked cast offs. Following Roger's example, Nathan knelt until motioned to rise.

Edward addressed Roger in French, assuming that the ragged individual in a mix of unsuitable scavenged armour would not understand. He asked for Nathan's identity and that of his commander and to whose contingent he was attached. Nathan surprised both men by butting in using semi-comprehensible schoolboy French. When the two aristocrats realised what their unusual visitor was saying, they reverted to speaking English.

Red faced and trying to bite chunks off a chicken drumstick, despite the efforts of the Steward to undress him, the King spoke calmly and clearly to his old ally. "You're bleeding Roger. It is unlike one of my best swordsmen to be skewered."

Roger gave a wave of dismissal, "He paid with his life, one of twelve I have killed who will oppose you no more your Majesty, and my new surgeon here has sewn me together quite perfectly. If I may, I will rest for a while but I really would like to know how goes the battle?"

The King, over six feet tall and well muscled, smacked him on the shoulder and eagerly replied, "It goes well in most parts of the battlefield. We had outrageous good fortune with the snow coming when it did, blowing into their faces. I believe it to be divine intervention and a great omen for the success of our cause. Our prayers this breakfast time were well chosen and delivered. In three parts of the field, we have broken the line and they are in retreat. Warwick has finally arrived with his army and they are desperate to join in. I hope there will be enough of the enemy left to give his troops some reward."

Nathan observed that the King had been heavily involved in the fighting. His shirt was soaked with sweat and the Steward peeled it off together with the long stockings and linen drawers, before providing new underwear, clean woollen hose and a long sleeved linen shirt. The king's torso and upper arms were marked with wheals and bruises, where adversaries had connected with glancing blows but his fighting skills and well fitting armour had saved him from serious injury. Throughout this undressing, the two commanders discussed the battle.

Sir Roger reported his own experiences. "I saw you at the head of the army as you gave the order to advance. I know Our Lord is with us in your leadership. It was a bold move and I am certain they were surprised. Our encounters in my section took us far to the left of the centre and I lost sight of you completely in the snowstorm." The two continued discussing what had happened on the battlefield.

As the Steward finished his duty, the King ordered Rodger to instruct his commanders to pursue the Lancastrians as they fled to York and reminded him that no quarter was to be offered. Nathan, initially spellbound in the Royal's presence, had recovered his ability to rationalise and his curiosity overcame his awe. When an opportunity occurred, he begged leave to ask a question. Edward looked at Rodger, who nodded, and Edward said, "Very well surgeon, but speak slowly in our native tongue, your accent confuses my ears."

Showing maximum respect in the words he chose, Nathan said that he believed knights were sworn to follow a strict code of chivalry and yet he had witnessed no mercy being given. The genial expression on the face of the king slowly changed and, when he answered, there was a steely resolve in his voice: "Today, this battle will see the end of the wars, which have divided the realm. In the past 25 years, many noble families have lost members, slain in battle. Until this year, the wealthy who surrendered were spared for ransom. Their families paid to get them home and then we faced the same men in the next battle. Well, we do not intend to leave any alive today. Chivalry, you say? My father, my brother and my uncle were ambushed at Wakefield in December whilst out foraging for food. Their heads are even now spiked on the gates of York. Chivalry is dead. There will be no quarter." He could have added that his father's head had been mocked with a paper crown but he could not speak of such humiliation. Nathan knew he had touched a raw nerve.

The Steward, who had paused while the King spoke, now helped him into a neatly fitting padded jacket, over which he strapped bespoke Italian plate armour. Once ready to re-join the fray, the King ordered Nathan to seek out wounded nobles and help them. As he left, he stuck out a fist and dug Nathan in the chest, "You are not afraid to speak out in your strange English. I may have a place for you at Court if you are able to swear loyalty to the Crown." Then, donning a thick woven skull cap and carrying his helmet, he strode off, a young man with the world at his feet and looking, in every detail, like a King. Nathan was so fascinated with his quiet authority, he momentarily forgot his own misfortune.

CHAPTER 13

Margaret was ill at ease. Although the chair was cushioned, she was restless and uncomfortable. Her view of the range of hills from the window of her room in the Scottish Highlands, only partially occupied her thoughts.

"What is he like?" she asked her friend, Mary of Gelderbrand. "What is Sir David Stirling's most attractive feature?"

Even though she was Queen Regent of Scotland and familiar with the frankness of those of high birth, Mary was surprised by the question.

"He is a most honourable man, My Lady. Well respected in the hunt and reported to be most kindly disposed to his household staff. I am told that hawking and stalking are his principal distractions."

Margaret persisted with her desire to find out something of her host's personality. "But how does he live? Does he own large estates? I see only mountains and moorland in this country. I have yet to see a farm with crops, all seem to be keeping cattle. Are there farms and has he wealth from his family?"

"I think you will find that Sir David has wealth enough to back your enterprise if he should be so disposed. Raising an army in France to help you to regain your throne – with the King of course – might well appeal to him. He has no love for the English. Where he leads, others will follow, I am sure."

It was Margaret's plan to reward her allies in Scotland with gifts of land taken from the Yorkists nobles, such as the town of Berwick, now gifted to Mary of Gelderbrand.

On the arrival of Henry's party in the northern most parts of England and in Scotland, news soon spread of the terrible death toll at Towton. The defeated King was, at first, much impressed by the sympathetic hospitality he and his family received from the Northern aristocracy and his Scottish allies. Although it became clear that every possible supporter wished to know the full details so that they might assess the implications of providing support for the deposed Henry and his queen. It soon became obvious to his sympathisers that his viewpoint was less about the misery of Towton and the loss of so many noblemen and supporters of the House of Lancaster, and more about England's inability to live in harmony with itself.

Henry's confessions of his own inability to unite the country made no reference to any desire to regain his throne, a sentiment emanating most strongly from the former queen. Rather than draw admiration for his honesty, his Scottish allies interpreted his demeanour as the excuses of a weak monarchy. Henry soon tired of the encounters with his Scottish supporters and retired quietly to the company of religious advisers. His diplomatic purpose was passed to Margaret, who accepted the responsibility with alacrity. She planned to use her contacts in the north of the country to help her get to France, where she might coax the King, her cousin, to help Henry regain the throne of England.

Margaret was no stranger to the Channel. A few years earlier, she had crossed to England in a violent storm and needed two weeks recuperation in Southampton before she was fit to face the marriage. Yet she was raised in an age when survival demanded that she did so. The exhilaration of her coronation was soon followed by the depressing realisation that her husband, King since his boyhood, was some way from being an inspirational leader of men. Henry exercised no control; he merely followed advice and delegated both decisions and actions. Margaret was astute enough to keep her views to herself but, from there on, her actions were always to do whatever she thought necessary to ensure her son's accession to the throne.

Henry's failure to apply a strong hand with Government, she reasoned, had led to the current situation, where he, she and her son were now fugitives in their own realm. Determined to pursue her plan, Margaret left her bewildered husband in the sanctuary of an abbey in Edinburgh and headed, with her son, to the coast in search of a passage. At Berwick she hired a trading boat to take her south to Northumberland before finding a sea captain at Bamborough prepared to carry her to Brittany. On the second day, the Prince developed high colour with profuse sweats. Margaret was assisted by only a single Lady-in-waiting, who spent most of the time looking after the Prince. The following day, the boy spent the whole time vomiting and it became clear he suffered from sea sickness like his mother. To escape from the smell and claustrophobia of the cabin,

Margaret spent as much daylight time as possible on deck, ruminating on the possible successful outcome of her journey. As the boat nosed through the Channel, each wave seemed to emphasise the challenges she had faced since her marriage. She resolved to secure the support of the French King, even if it meant promising to surrender all Crown territory in Calais.

CHAPTER 14

Two weeks later, a hundred sea miles down the coastline, one of King Edward's finest galleons docked at Calais and its elegant passengers were royally entertained by the English garrison. After a few days rest, the party selected the finest mounts from the garrison's stables and set out on the overland journey to the Court of the French king. Leading the emissaries was Roger of Launceston and in his retinue rode Nathan accompanied by Calvert, now elevated to the position of Steward and astride his own horse, having earned his promotion by his readiness to learn and support Nathan. He gathered grasses for the horses and puzzled about his dramatic change of circumstances. He was still mystified by Nathan. He knew nothing of the man's background and it puzzled him to think why he and his friends had discovered the man on the field at Towton.

After Towton, Nathan had quickly become a regular presence at the English Court, both for his knowledge of medicine and what was taken to be an ability to foresee the future. Except, he told himself wryly, his own. He had warned the King of Margaret's likely attempt to persuade her cousin to support her to regain the Crown of England. Nevertheless, he had been surprised to have been invited to take part in the mission, the purpose of which was to wreck Margaret's predicted attempt to involve the French. The plan was to present Nathan as an earl having great influence with landowners in Northern England and the Borders. He would claim, quite unjustifiably, that, should the French and Scots unite to attack England from the North, they would not only meet the armies of a strong monarch, but also implacable popular resistance.

In itself, it was not a factor that would deter Louis from an alliance with Scotland. Although it was one strand of a misinformation plan Edward had drawn up to dupe the French. He wanted them to believe he was reinforcing the garrisons at Calais and Burgundy as a preparation for reclaiming the Crown's former possessions in Gascony.

It was late summer and the French countryside enraptured all the Englishmen, offering the riders a buffet of ripening nuts, berries and fruits, in addition to the small game Calvert shot for the pot. At each halt, he contrived to wander off into the woodland and explore the habitat so different from his birthplace. He unslung the bow and quiver in the canvas bag hanging from his saddle, taking it with him on each stop. It was not strung for instant action but he could not forget how recently he had earned a living. He gathered lush grasses as a treat for his horse of which he was inordinately proud, and shot small game which he skinned and dressed for the cooks travelling with the party. However, Nathan was good to him and had made it possible for him to improve his station in life.

The guide on their journey from Calais, Gaston, a bow-legged individual with a slight stoop and long bushy hair, rode a steed with some of the characteristics of its rider. It was bony, which Nathan took to be due to its age rather than a lack of fodder. Together, horse and rider might have been the leaders of an impoverished band of pilgrims, rather than one entrusted to safely bring the party to the Court of the King of France. It was always when the column stopped to eat that Gaston joined them in conversation. Noticing the French guide's habit of joining the Englishmen at meals, Nathan took Calvert to one side and cautioned him to be careful of what he said as the guide might be able to understand English.

"You think he is spying on us?" asked Calvert.

"He may look simple enough but it is best to take no chances. Do not speak of what you know about our purpose when he is within hearing," he warned.

After five days of easy riding, emerging from heavy forestation, the party were now overlooking rolling countryside of southern Normandy. It was late afternoon and the low sun reflected from a magnificent white building in the distance. A great stone gateway stood a bowshot ahead and a lane lined with poplars led from this gate to the Chateau de Domfront. Labourers, at work with the curious long handled shovels of the French, were building a dyke which would feed a lake enhancing the view from the front rooms of the building. In the middle of the excavation, men were erecting a structure, fitting together dazzling blocks of cut marble. By their style of clothing and darker skins, Nathan deduced they were Italian craftsmen and that they were building an ornamental fountain, a skill for which their race was famous. Before the portals of the chateau, the land had recently been terraced. Gardens had been laid out and he guessed that the new King had put these radical improvements to the landscape in train. The chateau, now resembling a country house more than a castle, appeared many-roomed with at least three levels.

"I am told the King likes to boast that he has more than one hundred staff in this household and working on the estate," Roger assured Nathan. "It was built by a prince who died before its completion and Charles, then Dauphin, acquired if for less than its real value. Unlike an English castle, it was not destined primarily for defence and could not hold out for long under siege." Nathan thought the conically topped towers at each corner suggested some capability for resistance. To the right, attached to the chateau, a long single storey wing stretched twenty metres. Apparently newly built, its external walls were decorated with mosaics featuring images of sea birds and fish. The king had obviously added a bathing house, the latest idea in luxury. Would they get to use it, Nathan mused? In contrast, nobody seemed to bother much about personal hygiene at the Court of Edward in London and he had found that keeping himself clean was a permanent struggle. It amused Calvert to observe the frequency with which his employer laundered his clothes.

At the lightly fortified portals of the main building, the English party was met by the King's Chamberlain and then guided by household staff through exquisitely tiled corridors to their rooms. Each room through which they passed was luxuriously decorated with walls in deep red and woodwork in gold. There were extravagant painting of both individuals and landscapes, several showing animals being hunted by men on horseback. Wild boar, deer and wolves were the main quarry. Between admiring the plasterwork relief of the ceilings and rich drapery decorating its many windows, Nathan attempted to engage his guide, a middle aged woman, in her own language. Yet, either she didn't understand his accent or had been ordered not to speak with him. Having shown him to an attractive room on the first floor, she then led Calvert to the rear of the palace where the servants slept.

CHAPTER 15

On their way to the Great Hall, where the first meeting was to take place, Roger told Nathan that Louis X1, recently crowned following the death of his father, Charles, Margaret's uncle, was a negotiator of considerable talent. He was known as 'the spider king', reflecting his habitual and rapid changes of direction when discussing matters of State and had been involved in many dubious negotiations when he was Dauphin. Years earlier, he had offered to support the Yorkist claim to the English throne but circumstances had changed.

When the French king met the Yorkist ambassador now, Roger took the initiative and delivered a favourable account of the battle at Towton. He then informed Louis that Parliament had, afterwards, attainted all Margaret's lands and those of the Prince of Wales. This thrust was designed to remove any notion that the French king might harbour that support for Margaret could bring attractive territorial advantages. The discussions were conducted in a mixture of English and Old French and Nathan was obliged to seek explanations on several occasions. During a break in the proceedings, Nathan conveyed to Rodger his belief that it would be unsafe to accept any Louis promise but another of Rodger's advisers took a different view. William Waldebrand was an interesting individual. He had fought for Edward at Towton and had witnessed the arrival of Nathan at the Saxton church sanctuary away from the battlefield and his ready acceptance by Edward into the Court. He had also watched Nathan's advisory role grow and his reputation become fixed in the minds of those nearest to the King.

Waldebrand had been long in the House of York as a loyal supporter of Edward's father and had fought alongside him at Wakefield, where he had been lucky to escape with his life. Now he agreed that the French monarch would not wish to back Margaret as she was penniless. All the lands she had possessed had been taken over by Edward. Instead, Louis might be inclined to support Edward if, instead of threatening to build up English armies in France, some offer of England's territories were put on the table as bargaining points. It was an astute approach but one which raised a few questions in Nathan's mind.

After a lengthy conference with no resolution, Waldebrand made sure he was next to Nathan as they withdrew from the Great Hall. Choosing his moment when they were out of hearing of the others, he asked Nathan if he would accompany him to a chamber where one of the party was suffering a stomach sickness. Nathan explained that he was not a "physic" and had no talent for divining "the humours", often held to be the cause of sickness at the time. Even so he agreed to see the man. On arrival at the chamber in another part of the palace, he was astonished to see an elegant woman with a young child. The velvet of her gown and her graceful movements told him she was of noble blood. Her face was familiar, as was the way she moved and, albeit with a French accent, the way she spoke. Then Nathan realised why.

He studied her closely as she instructed a nursemaid to put the child to bed in an adjoining room. As she spoke, an image entered the recesses of his brain of a woman in a different dimension, a distant reality. The lady came towards them and offered her hand, palm down. Unthinkingly, he bent over, took it in his and kissed it. Waldebrand jumped forward and shouldered him aside before kneeling at the woman's feet.

"Don't worry William, I take no insult," she said gently. Her sweet and low voice, with her charming French accent, was clear and her dark green eyes engaged Nathan's with a suggestion of amusement. She dismissed Waldebrand, who reluctantly accepted her request that he leave, and gestured for Nathan to sit. Then she spoke again.

"I am not sick and I apologise for getting you here under false pretences. Waldebrand says you are a wise man and soothsayer rather than a soldier," she said.

Nathan was unused to flattery and missed the warning signs. He was also partly consumed by a strange thought that he had encountered this attractive lady sometime before. Yet he couldn't think when or how. He made no move to increase the distance between them as she came to sit next to him on the chaise.

"I thought you might carry a personal message from me to Edward," she said, placing one of her hands on his forearm, "but can I trust you?" Nathan should have been suspicious as those entrancing eyes looked him up and down before engaging his own with unsettling steadiness. Was she flirting with him? He felt himself wanting to help her.

"I will help if I can but I must inform Rodger of Launceston as he is my mentor with the King," he said.

The lady looked at him steadily, assessing the risk she was about take and the vulnerability of the man she had chosen to trust.

"I am Margaret of Anjou. I am the wife of Henry, your true King," she said simply.

CHAPTER 16

Nathan was staggered. His instinct was to tell this lady that he was unable to help her and that Waldebrand had made a terrible mistake deluding her. He was also tempted to tell her that he was a fraud, a man caught up in circumstances over which he had no control, a man from another universe. Although events were complicated enough. This woman was the double of the girl he had fallen for in another universe before his destiny shot him back to the Middle Ages. Seeing his confusion, Margaret pressed her case, "You cannot tell Sir Roger. It would compromise his mission here were he to know that I am under the same roof. King Louis is my cousin."

Nathan knew that it was so but pretended he did not. He was slipping into the role of a spy without intending to do so. Waldebrand was apparently playing a dual role and could not be trusted. What should he do? He could take advice from no one. If he were to be found in this chamber, alone with the deposed Queen of England, the wrong interpretation might be placed on it. He decided to take the risk.

"What is the important matter you have in mind?" he finally asked. "Tell me and I will see if I can give you any advice."

Margaret tilted her head and coyly clasped her manicured hands. She was close enough for him to inhale the sweet herbal intensity of her perfume: "I wish to return. England is my home. I do not wish to live in Scotland or France any longer."

Nathan considered the implications. If this lady returned to England, she would still command support from the landowning nobility in the

North. If she were to have Scotland and France behind her, she would be a real threat to Edward. If she only wanted to raise her son in England, she could petition Edward to name the Prince of Wales as his successor. That might maintain peace in the realm. However, he was no politician and no match for the beguiling woman before him.

"You are homesick for England?" he asked, immediately recognising the naivety of his question.

"I want my son to be raised in England and to be loved by the whole country. I want him to grow into a fine gentleman," she paused, "and to inherit the Crown after Edward's reign." So, he was right, it was really about the line of succession. How could it harm anybody's interests if he, Nathan the surgeon, carried a message direct to the King's ear? After all, the King could either ignore the message or he could choose to act upon it. It wasn't as though they were planning treason.

"Alright, I will take your message, but I will be putting myself in a difficult position if I do not tell Sir Rodger what I have agreed to do." Nathan argued that he could delay telling Rodger until they had left the palace and were well on their way back to England but Margaret became animated. She said that in order for the message to be uncontaminated by politics, Nathan must deliver it himself. Intoxicated by the irresistible combination of her intellect and beauty, his resistance faded. Against his better judgement, he agreed.

Margaret rose to her feet, which he noticed were bare, and he wondered about that as she walked around the room untying the cords which held back drapes over the windows. With only the light from the fire in the grate illuminating the chamber, she returned to sit beside him on the chaise. She had light brown hair and a dark complexion with a straight nose and full mouth. Yet it was her grey eyes which captivated him most. Placing her hands on his shoulders, she brought her face close to his and smiled. She was strikingly pretty and a perfume of woodland flowers enhanced her appeal. Their first kiss was a chaste contact but her moist warm lips promised a great deal more. She disengaged before telling him, "I am not an ungrateful woman, demure is for state occasions – let me show you how French ladies kiss," and she placed her hands behind his head and, as their lips met, darted her tongue into his mouth. Slowly, Nathan subsided as she pressed her body into his, until he was lying on the raised cushion of the chaise.

She stood and took several dainty steps backwards, never taking her eyes off his. Then, holding her gown with a hand at each side, she gradually raised it until the hemline was level with her throat. Nathan saw that lingerie did not feature in the wardrobe of mediaeval women. She was hungry for the act and eager to create a memory Nathan would wish to relive for the rest of his life. She knelt before him, her hands busy and practised. He had never known this kind of lovemaking and, at first, resisted her attempts. Though he was soon lying back with her fingers deep inside his mouth, smothering his gasped appeals for her to stop.

An hour later and with many new sensual experiences behind him, Nathan tried to raise the subject of the woman's relationship with the deposed King of England.

"Henry is my husband but has never been a real man to me," she told him. "When he is not wandering in his mind, he is married to his religion and communications with the saints."

"But your son, the Prince of Wales? He is by all accounts a fine boy?" Nathan phrased the question diplomatically.

"Yes, I am pleased to say my son is taking after his father," she replied with an enigmatic smile.

CHAPTER 17

Nathan decided to return to his own room and, to avoid drawing anyone's attention, he left by a side door. Orientating himself, he passed along a corridor to the rear of the building and, opening a door he thought might take him into the palace grounds, he found himself with a noisy group of senior members of the Household, enjoying their wine. Seated with them was the guide, Gaston. The Frenchman looked up and his smile melted as he recognised the Englishman. Nathan apologised for his intrusion and quickly turned and left, closing the door. I am right he thought, if he isn't a paid spy, he is certainly very friendly with the palace staff.

Daylight drew him to another door, which was open and gave him access to the grounds. He saw he had emerged at the rear of the palace, where he found acres of parkland with enchanting footpaths surrounded by formal avenues of trees. The air was like chilled champagne. It was late summer and the sun heightened the colouring of the foliage. Above the treetops, rooks disputed ownership of the airspace, their raucous arguments a tonic to his senses. The vegetation was fresh and delicately scented. He pushed back his head, stared up to the sky and inhaled the purity of the season. Then, drawn in the clear blue sky, he saw the vapour trail of an aircraft. It took a split second before he realised its significance. Vapour trail? Jet travel? He was back to reality. He stared at the sky and now realised that it was an illusion. Simply a thin white cloud cruelly dispersed into elongated tracery.

Demoralised, he quickly calmed himself and decided that at least it was positive proof he really did belong in another century. His knew life had become a parody of what he had read of the Middle Ages, now manifested in a sequence of dreams. He promised himself he must hold firmly to the belief in his eventual return to the 21st Century.

He decided to talk to Calvert, not in too much depth but sufficient to secure a different perspective on matters affecting their relationship. He made his way to the rear of the palace, where he found the Steward's quarters. He wondered if he dare share some superficial knowledge of his new mission for Margaret of Anjou. Calvert was proving himself and alert and quick witted young man and Nathan had no doubt that, had he received an education, he would have climbed the social ladder. Despite having lived through the hell of Towton and despatched several of the enemy, there was innocence about him and he knew only to tell the truth. This had made him an ideal Steward to Nathan, but could he, in any way, help with understanding Nathan's personal quandary?

"Do you find yourself wondering what is happening at home?" he asked. "Will your family be safe while you are absent?"

Calvert swallowed a mouthful of the wine and considered his answer. "I left them all the plunder and the wages I was paid for fighting. My brothers and sisters work in the fields and we keep good terms with our landlord. They should be alright. I do miss them. But what of your family? You never speak of them."

That is a good question; Nathan thought to himself and had to weigh up carefully how he answered, "I have no real family. There are friends I miss. Why do you ask? Do I seem strange to you, perhaps like a person from a foreign country?"

"Yes, that is so. Apart from the strange clothes you wore when we came across you lying on the field at Towton, many times afterwards I discussed with Goodrich how you came to be at the battle. We felt you did not expect to be there and you were not there to fight as were we."

"The truth is Calvert I have no idea how I came to be there or how I might return to my real home. I awoke lying in the snow with a dead horse on top of me. If you had not found me, I would have frozen to death. I now try to explain my situation by thinking some evil wizard had cast a spell over me and transported me to the battlefield. But what I might have done to incur the wrath of a wizard, I have no answer."

Nathan went on to talk about the civil strife in England and those battles he knew as the Wars of the Roses; he tried to give Calvert an overall picture of the problems of mediaeval England and the rivalry between the house of York and Lancaster. He was careful to give both points of view and he thought that this might be the best approach for his next piece of information.

"I want to share a secret with you, Calvert and you must swear to tell no one. None of the emissaries know what I am about to tell you. Can you hear and then keep my secret?"

He watched Calvert's face change from curiosity to puzzlement before adding, "I have agreed to carry a message from Margaret of Anjou to King Edward. she is living here in the palace but she longs for peace to come to the realm at home."

Calvert's mouth opened and he stuttered, "But she is our enemy. You told me she was the leader of the enemy army at Towton."

"She was indeed. But you will not see the end of demands to go and risk your life fighting fellow Englishmen until we have a stable monarchy and there is lasting agreement between the Houses of York and Lancaster. Please trust me as I trust you and say nothing of this to anyone. I will deliver the message to King Edward and let him be the judge of whether she is sincere about wanting only peace. Do you promise to keep my secret?"

Calvert agreed but appeared mystified and Nathan wondered if he might have taken a step too far with the lad's trust.

CHAPTER 18

There was no knock on the door. It imploded and four armed men charged in. Nathan thought he was about to be murdered but they dragged him from the bed and frogmarched him down the stairs of his lodgings into the yard. Here, he was laid across a horse with his wrists tied to his feet under the belly of the animal. In this position he was transported through the streets of London to the Tower.

The dungeon was cold and damp and having been left there without food or drink for a day, Nathan was at the extreme end of miserable. He had been imprisoned in his current persona for so long that now he often doubted his identity. Was he locked in a trance or was this his true life? Were the images he held of shooting grouse on a Yorkshire Moor a memory, or the unique clairvoyance of a disordered brain? Paradoxically, his mind was breaking up under the stress of living the deceit he needed to remain sane. As the 21st Century became increasingly remote in his thoughts, his confusion over his identity grew. He was an espionage agent living in an occupied territory, forever submerged in artificial existence. He had been awaiting an audience with King Edward, staying in a half respectable inn on the banks of the Thames.

The individual who entered the dungeon was real enough. He wore the Royal insignia of York and his face told its own story. He was hard, he was ugly and he was cruel. A limp gave his movements a sinister dimension and his half smile remained glacially set.

"So," he began, "the man without a past. How are you feeling? Are you ready to tell me who you really are and why you have been involved in treason, or do you wish me to introduce you to my toolbox?"

Nathan thought his heart would stop. He was powerless with only his wits to protect him and he felt he was rapidly losing those. "I must see Rodger of Launceston, " he begged.

"But he does not wish to see you," replied the gaoler. "He disowns you. We know about your treachery with the French she-wolf," he said, his voice a grating rasp of hate.

Nathan gasped. Calvert was implicated and he rued his carelessness in revealing his meeting with Margaret. He was sure the lad wished him no harm and that he would have been tricked into disclosing Nathan's meeting in France. He prayed that no injury had come to him as a result.

The filthy fingernails of his inquisitor's hands dug into his wrists and Nathan was forced to his feet. The man spun him around and expertly tied both hands behind his back.

"I'm taking you for some exercise. Somewhere you're not going to like." He pushed his prisoner through the door of the cell into a dank passage with little light. Halfway along, he kicked open another door and pushed Nathan through. It was the torture chamber, furnished with an array of the most obscene tools and apparatus that the twisted minds of madmen could devise. Instinctively, Nathan threw himself backwards into his captor. Yet the reaction was expected and he encountered only a pair of strong hands, braced to arrest the move.

As he was barged into the chamber, Nathan noticed for the first time two ghoul-like individuals with blank faces. They came forward and strapped him into a solid timber chair stained with dark red patches. Terrified, Nathan immediately offered to tell them all they might want to know about his meeting with Margaret.

"It is not treason," he blurted, "Margaret wants to come back to live in England and I was asked to tell the king. That was what she asked me to do. Please allow me to do so."

The inquisitor held up his hand: "Shut up, you need to learn the system here. It is this. First we inflict the pain and afterwards we ask the questions. I have no interest in anything you say before you have suffered."

"I'm telling you the truth now. You can't torture me. You'd be wasting your time. I can only tell you the same."

"They all say that, but you would be surprised how different their stories can be after they have experienced the benefits of my unusual craft."

The inquisitor smiled as he selected a knotted rope tourniquet and place it over Nathan's head. He took great care to position the knots where they would guarantee most pain. Then he twisted the wooden handle and the tourniquet tightened. His voice became muffled and indistinct. Not for the first time in his dual existence, Nathan was convinced he was about to die.

CHAPTER 19

The doors of the elevator opened and the single occupant stepped out, tutting when he was obliged to step around the person standing stock still in front of the lift doors. Nathan barely registered the arrival of the elevator. Instead of sliding steel doors, he saw a rough timber door, cross braced for strength. Through it, three ghostly faces peered at him. Three ghouls wielding tools for gouging eyes, crushing teeth and fracturing bones. He was paralysed, unable to step into the lift. His clenched fists beat against his thighs and he choked when he tried to speak.

Then, from behind him, a familiar female voice broke through his trance. "Are you getting in?" she asked, "is something the matter?"

The person walked around him and entered the elevator. Nathan fought to make his brain take in his surroundings. He moved aside and then realised he must have intended to ride the elevator. He stepped inside after the woman and, at that moment, an electric shock jolted him into reality. The woman turned to face Nathan, her green eyes breaking into a smile of recognition.

"What are you doing here? Are you involved in the meeting? You soon changed your mind. I thought you said you were off back to England," Koley began.

"I wasn't...I don't know..." his reply faded as he sought to grasp his translocation from mediaeval England. It was too much. He must seem stupid, not knowing what to say but otherwise appearing normal. He had to find out what was happening to him. Questions crowded his mind but one came before all others. He looked into Koley's alluring eyes and was unable to stop himself asking "What year is it?"

"What year? Are you serious? What a bloody question! I don't know what game you're playing but forget it. I have to prepare for an important meeting. I thought you must have returned to England. We all did. We couldn't find you. You left no contact details." Koley's tone was sad and in her voice Nathan sensed the resentment at having felt she had been dumped.

"Yes, I'm back. Well, I was. ...I don't know.." He stopped as his brain didn't seem to function and he knew he was incoherent. Then, looking for safer ground, he asked, "How's the launch going?"

Koley froze and her face showed her astonishment."You haven't heard? My God, where have you been? Cyrus Blatt is dead. Car crash last weekend. The entire programme's in chaos. You were nowhere to be found."

Nathan took in the new information without emotion. Compared to what he had been through in the past few… the past what? How many days? He had no idea. He had lived a few years in the Middle Ages but seemed to be back in the present where only a few days had elapsed.

"Who's taken over the launch? You?"

Koley nodded: "Scaife Sciences are coming out with a rival system which is reported to offer exactly what we have."

Nathan showed his surprise. "I thought Neuro-Praxis was miles ahead of any competition. They have been extremely smart to catch up so quickly - if they have caught up."

"They have," she said. "Their CEO was in touch with Sal Goering when news of Blatt's death broke. Apparently he offered a joint marketing agreement and said enough about the system to emphasise where they are at. They are almost ready to go."

Nathan withdrew into his business mind. He asked himself how Scaife had managed to carry out the development work in less time than Bagnold. It was impossible, even if they had enjoyed some lucky discoveries instead of grinding out trial and error testing, unless... somehow they had gained possession of the Neuro-Praxis manuals kept under strict security at Bagnold. As he worked through the situation in his head, his mind became clearer. He slowly considered each member of the launch team, looking for signs that might give some clue. Cyrus Blatt? But he was dead. Perhaps it wasn't an accident. Perhaps he had been blackmailed? What about the in-house trouble-shooters, Mogdanowicz and Seimens? They must have felt they had had their noses pushed out when the top management had brought in an Englishman to solve the problems they were grappling with? All the scenarios played out in Nathan's mind. Finally, he decided he would advise Sal Goering that on no account should he consider a joint marketing or any other type of deal with Scaife until he had investigated further.

I'll start with Blatt, he thought. I never liked the bully. We need to go through his files. Has anybody looked through his desk since he died?

Koley fixed up hotel accommodation and, the following day, Nathan was at the police department in an interview with a senior member of traffic police. The Officer said he was trying to work out what had happened and there was a possibility of a charge against the driver of the truck which had hit Blatt on the wrong side of the road. Although it had been difficult to align the truck driver's version of events with the actuality of the crash.

"There was some snow around that night and Mr Blatt's Jaguar showed he was using all the safety features fitted in the vehicle, including traction control and, obviously, dipped headlights. The truck driver said he thought the road was clear until the Jaguar suddenly appeared before him with headlights blazing. There had been hardly any snow and the road was dry." The Officer said one or other of the two drivers had completely mistaken the conditions but the truck driver was adamant that he had taken no risks. No suggestion of alcohol having been involved was ever raised. Nathan decided that it would be a waste of time trying to make progress with his enquiries by becoming involved in the details of the accident and he would prefer to dig into the facts surrounding Blatt's extraordinary financial gain. It wasn't difficult to check with the foreign bank on Blatt's newly deposited fortune. It was traced back to the Cayman Island and to Scaife Science.

Nathan knew what needed to be done. Organised at breakneck speed, Bagnold funded a spectacular launch of the new software. It unfolded in several capital cities at the same time and brought the awareness of Neuro-Praxis to a vast audience. Nathan elected to be present at the New York event, where he could stay on for a few days afterwards and meet up with Koley on her return from the Brisbane launch. It was shortly after the launch, as Bagnold's management were congratulating themselves on the terrific response of the target market that Nathan began to worry about the possibility that Scaife had somehow sneaked a lead in the race for sales. To everyone's astonishment, there had been no reaction from them to the worldwide launch. They remained silent. None of the business media carried interviews containing comment – neither favourable nor otherwise. Nathan was not the only one to find this extraordinary. He clinched a meeting with Bagnold's CEO and let the chief know his mind.

Goering protested, "What the devil is wrong with you Nathan? You've piloted a tremendously successful launch and you can return to England with your reputation enhanced, your pockets stuffed with dollars and get back to shooting grouse. You don't need to stay with the team here. You've done a great job."

"Thanks Sal. But before I leave, would you authorise me to take a final trip into the neural pathways? I can check that all is working as we hoped."

"God dammit man. Take a look-see if you must and if the surgeon thinks it holds no risks for you. I'm sure it will be plain sailing. The software is working so smoothly. But do it if you must. One last time. "

Nathan cleared his intended immersion into Neuro-Praxis with the surgeon who had helped him previously. He didn't try to cut any corners. He went through the same preparatory procedures he had negotiated several times before. When he took Koley into his confidence about his plan, she tried to talk him out of it but his mind was set.

"The element of danger is much less than when I did this the first time – before we had learned what we now know. It will be perfectly safe for me. I should be 'hooked up' for less than a couple of hours unless I encounter a problem that needs fixing - which I doubt."

The brain surgeon was invited to be present and several senior personnel also gathered. Recordings were to be made of any information Nathan gave out whilst connected to the system and the atmosphere in the surgery on the day was more like a meeting of the marketing personnel than a hospital procedure.

Nathan lay on a surgical bed as his head was wired to the computer, the latest model and deemed perfect to employ the Neuro-praxis software. It all seemed like a re-run of some of the presentations used at the launch. Then, quite slowly, the tone of Nathan's voice began to change as his brain followed the neural pathways. Koley, in the front row of the bystanders, noticed it first and a loud intake of breath signalled her fear. "Something's going wrong," she exclaimed, in an alarmed tone.

CHAPTER 20

Nathan Chalmers awoke with a sickening headache lying in a four-poster bed. The covers were of a luxurious material embroidered with intricate flower patterns. They were heavy and hindered his attempts to sit upright to take stock. He smacked himself on his cheeks to focus his mind and, with almost imperceptible pace, he began to recognise his surroundings. He had been here before, transported to the heart of a foreign country many years ago as part of a mission to negotiate with the King of France. Slowly he allowed his gaze to traverse the room in which he lay. As he became gradually alert, he realised with a monumental shock It was the bedroom of Margaret of Anjou, one time Queen of England, the woman into whose service he had been seduced. Through the fog of an incomplete memory, he recalled the terrifying experience of being imprisoned in a medieval torture chamber and the heart stopping vision of grinning torturer leaning over him with a pair of giant pliers.

Waking from a dream of a romantic evening with Koley, Nathan was unsure of his whereabouts. He drew the bed covers tighter around his neck, shuffling his feet together to try to inject warmth. He thought to get out of bed to find extra blankets enough to lift the temperature sufficiently to allow him to go back to sleep. Sleep was his obsession. Why was it so cold? He decided to leave the unsatisfactory charm of the bed and put on some clothes. A decent breakfast and some coffee should put a different complexion on the day.

It was only at that point did he realise he was not in the room Koley had organised for him at the hotel. In fact, he was not in any room he had ever seen before. It was quite small, had no artistic merit and smelt more like a kitchen than a bedroom. Slowly now, but with gathering conviction, he realised he was in a ship's cabin. Suddenly, his surroundings were illuminated by a dim light. Then the light faded for a few seconds before returning much brighter. There was a constant low hammering outside his room. He lurched to the door and dragged it open. What he saw drew him back and he staggered onto his unmade bed. The corridor outside was crowded with passengers in different stages of undress, all of whom appeared to be attempting to run in the same direction. There were no shouts or screams but all seemed to be speaking at one and the same time. They were pushing the people before them crowded in an unholy queue. It was bedlam.

Nathan snatched up a pair of trousers and jacket before returning to the door and grabbing the handle. He tried to open it but the something had changed and it stuck halfway open. It refused to yield enough space for him to get out. He had to struggle with it with some violence before he could escape. He joined the throng in the corridor shouting, "What the hell's going on?" Nevertheless, as everyone seemed to be asking the same questions, he grew no wiser.

For ten interminable minutes he fought his way forward in the struggling mass of humanity heading up several staircases before emerging into the cold night air on what he believed to be escape. Here, the scene was no clearer and the explanation still out of reach.

A figure in mariner's uniform cannoned into him before grabbing his arm and bellowing "You'll do, come with me". He was still completely ignorant of his location.

The night was ice cold and the dark on which he now found himself was crowded with unsuitably clad people. More women than men he thought.

The starless night sky gave no clue to his whereabouts and he blundered along with the mariner maintaining a vice like grip on his upper arm. They barged through knots of people of both sexes, hugging each other as if in some kind of party and arrived at a point where other mariners were marshalling the panic stricken throng into a semblance of order.

Nathan, now fully awake but enveloped in a sea of ignorance, recognised the extraordinary scenario displayed before him. His instinct was to discuss the problem he watched develop but conversation was impossible. The sailor now let go of his arm to seize a weeping women clad in what seemed like her nightdress. As the sailor took hold of her, she threw her arms around his neck in frenzy and wrestled him against the ship's rails. His cap was knocked to the ground and Nathan bent to retrieve it. Sailors knew the important role their caps played in establishing their authority. As Nathan handed the peaked cap to its owner, he caught the name in gold thread above the peek. The sharp lettering spelt out the name of his ship.... TITANIC.

The end

ACKNOWLEDGEMENTS

I am grateful for the interest and support of several people equipped with technical expertise outside my own areas of knowledge. Without their help I could have produced a much less authoritative version of events.

Iain Scott Caldwell

Moira Stewart Cooper

Tom Montgomery

Cleo Watson.

JOHN COOPER

John Cooper is a Yorkshireman living in Scarborough, who has broad experience of writing in different genres. He is a former national newspaper journalist, now a playwright and poet. He trained as a journalist aged 19 and subsequently had a long career on newspapers, eventually on the staff of the Daily Express. He set up a public relations consultancy in the 1970's and was retained by many national companies and institutions, including Ranks Hovis McDougal, Portakabin, British Sugar, Great Ormond Street Hospital, and Burmah Engineering. He advised Leeds Metropolitan University on the setting up of a degree course in public relations in the 1990's and has lectured on aspects of public relations to institutes of tertiary education.

He has written numerous sketches for revues presented by amateur societies and has a catalogue of plays, several of which have been staged by the Outreach Department of the Stephen Joseph Theatre. In his professional career, he has written the creative treatments, narrations and shooting scripts for promotional films and documentaries. He has read his poetry and short stories at literary festivals and other events.

In 2012 he was awarded an Honours Degree in Creative Writing by the University of Hull. A collection of poetry, "UNRELIABLE JUDGEMENTS", was published in 2010 and is held in public libraries in Yorkshire. In 2016 a collection of his mainly humorous short stories was published under the title "TALES OF THE CURIOUSLY UNFORTUNATE". His work has appeared in several poetry anthologies, magazines and newspapers.

"Fields of Madness" is his first novel.

www.ingramcontent.com/pod-product-compliance
Ingram Content Group UK Ltd.
Pitfield, Milton Keynes, MK11 3LW, UK
UKHW021829270726
14058UKWH00001B/55